MAHALIA

ALSO AVAILABLE FROM DELL LAUREL-LEAF BOOKS

MAHALIA

Joanne Horniman

Published by
Dell Laurel-Leaf
an imprint of
Random House Children's Books
a division of Random House, Inc.
New York

Visit us on the Web! www.randomhouse.com/teens

Educators and librarians, for a variety of teaching tools, visit us at www.randomhouse.com/teachers

ISBN: 0-440-23789-0

RL: 5.9

Reprinted by arrangement with Alfred A. Knopf

Printed in the United States of America

First Dell Laurel-Leaf Edition December 2004

10 9 8 7 6 5 4 3 2 1

OPM

Now the man has a child
He knows all the names
of the local dogs.
— Japanese poem

Matt loved Mahalia. He loved the smell of her, of fresh soft skin and milky sleepiness. He loved her bald vulnerable head, and the tender folds of skin on her neck. He loved her tiny fingers that clutched at his clothing and folded themselves up into fists when she slept. He loved the way she sucked intensely at her bottle and gazed at him with her crosseyed stare. Most of all he loved the fact of her. He loved her because she existed.

On a windy August day that threatened rain, when Mahalia was exactly five months, three weeks, and three days old, and Matt was seventeen and a half, he stood by the side of the road holding her against his chest in a cloth pouch, swaying his body gently to and fro to soothe her as she slept. He gazed down at her. Her skin was almost transparent, and expressions played across her sleeping face the way cloud shadows chase each other across a landscape. Matt felt the calm movement of his chest as he breathed, and the answering movement of Mahalia's body.

He stood beside the road heading north out of Lismore till almost midday, waiting to hitch out of town. Most of his possessions—three plastic garbage bags and a guitar—sat beside him, and he waited patiently, knowing it was simply a matter of time until someone stopped to give him a lift.

Lismore was an old town built on a slow brown river whose banks were choked by weeds and vines. On the hills above the town and stretching out toward the coast crept a brick-and-tile suburbia, but here, where Matt waited, were mostly high-set old timber houses. Their stumps and aging weatherboard were askew; they had suffered a hundred years of relentless sunlight and regular floods, and somehow still stood.

An old Toyota Corona pulled up beside Matt and a young man motioned for him to get in. He never spoke as he took them on a winding road through weed-infested farmland and rainforest remnants to a village called The Channon, where Matt only had to wait fifteen minutes before a woman in an old Holden station wagon picked him up.

"You've got a beautiful baby," said the woman as the car moved off, spraying gravel and spinning the wheels. Mahalia flinched at the sound but stayed asleep.

"Thank you," said Matt. He looked down at Mahalia and smiled.

"How far do you want to go?"

"Mount Nardi. Almost to the top?"

"That's where I'm going. You're in luck. Whose place?"

"Julie Mitchell's. You know her?"

"Sure do. I'm just a few places before hers. You must be her son, Matt. And this must be Mahalia. My name's Therese. I've lived down the road from your mum for a couple of months."

Matt smiled at her; he didn't mind that she already knew

2

about him. That was what it was like when you lived in the bush: everyone knew everyone.

The Holden crunched gears and proceeded uphill. Car bodies lay abandoned by the roadside; the road up Mount Nardi killed transmissions. They wound up through the rainforest, and the air became cooler, and moister, until they were driving into light cloud. Finally, when it seemed that the old car could bear no further punishment, they were at the driveway of Matt's mother's place.

Mahalia woke as he got out of the car, opening her eyes suddenly and staring at his face. Matt waited for the sound of the engine to recede before he made a move. He wanted to savor the silence, which wasn't real silence but the sounds of the bush. If you listened, there was life going on all around you.

"Hey, Mahalia, hey," he said, jiggling her softly in the cloth pouch. She looked into his eyes; she had the most direct gaze of anyone he knew.

It started to rain lightly, so Matt left the garbage bags in the drive for the moment, caught the handle of the guitar case in one hand, steadied Mahalia with the other, and made his way up to the house.

His mother was on the veranda. "I thought I heard a car." She smiled and held out her arms for the baby. Matt undid the strap of the carry pouch and released Mahalia into the waiting arms. He turned around without a word and went back for his things.

"Where's Emmy?" called his mother.

"Emmy's gone away for a while," he said when he'd returned with the garbage bags and dumped them on the floor of the living room. He looked into his mother's face. "I don't know if she'll come back." It was the first time he'd expressed his fear aloud. He sat down at the table.

Mahalia started to cry. It was her hungry cry. Matt got to his feet and rummaged in his bag for her bottle. "Have you got any boiled water?"

"There's probably some in the kettle. Look, I'll do it."

"No! *I* can." He dumped the bottle and a can of formula on the bench.

After Mahalia had been fed and was sleeping again on a blanket on the floor, his mother said, "What happened with Emmy?"

"Happened? Nothing. She wanted to get away. She said it was getting too much for her—the baby, and me, and . . . everything, I suppose. She said she was going to stay with a friend of her mother's in Sydney, a sort of godmother or something. She gets on better with the godmother than she does with her mum. So she got on the bus and—went."

"When?"

"A week ago."

"I see." His mother nodded, weighing what he'd said. She didn't look surprised, and Matt felt in some obscure way that he'd disappointed her.

"Why do you think she mightn't be back?" she asked in her quiet, reasonable voice. She was a social worker. She observed people's lives falling apart all the time.

"She took all her stuff. And . . . I don't know, just a feeling I have sometimes. But she wouldn't leave Mahalia forever—would she?"

He looked at his mother, who held his gaze for a moment and

then got up and moved over to the sink. She wiped it carefully with the sponge, her head bowed, then turned to face him.

"You know you can stay here as long as you like," she said. "You're not on your own—you know that."

When Mahalia woke, Matt took her out into the garden, upending her and carrying her firmly upside down, her body secure against his chest. He'd carried her like this for short periods almost since she was born. He'd heard somewhere it would help her spatial development, whatever that was. The way she experienced spaces, or something. Matt wanted Mahalia to experience all the spaces of the world, fully. She looked out at the world upside down with a solemn expression, her little mouth shaped into an O, her eyes round too. She was so calm and alert that he knew she liked being carried this way.

He took her to the looking-out spot, a cleared place that overlooked the forested valley. Matt was sure there wasn't a better place in the world. Wind had blown the cloud away now.

"Look at that view, Mahalia," he said. "Just look." He knew she couldn't see into the distance, but he hoped the beauty would seep into her bones.

Next, he walked her round inside the house, right way up this time. Up close, she could see very well. She noticed everything. The whole world was new and full of wonder for her.

He took her into the room his mother used as a studio and showed her the masks made of leather and papier-mâché.

"What do you think of this one?" he asked, showing her a mask with a smiling face, red cheeks, and yellow woolen braids. Mahalia waved her arm at it and tried to reach out and take hold of it. She babbled and smiled.

5

He moved on to a stern-faced leather mask with hard high cheekbones and black eyebrows. Mahalia creased her face into a scowl and began to bellow.

"Oh, no, no, it won't hurt you!" said Matt, taking her quickly away to show her a mobile of bright satin fish that hung in front of the window. "Look, Mahalia, little fishies, like the ones Grannie made *you*. A red one and a green one and a blue one and a purple one." Matt touched each fish as he spoke, and they bounced about. Mahalia stopped crying and reached out to touch them.

When he was little, Matt and his mother had collected shells and brought them home, where they still smelled deliciously of the sea. They looked up books to find out the names. There were cart-rut shells, fine white angel's wings, and shells that they called *hats*, which were a kind of limpet. There were scallop shells, and zebra volutes, and turban shells, and cat's eyes. There was the occasional rare cowrie.

His mother collected everything. She collected beautiful fabric and lace and trimmings in different colors and textures, which she used to make quilts or wall hangings or mobiles; and building materials, which she had gradually made into a house for them. She collected a lot of stuff that seemed like rubbish too: electrical wire, and old wooden soft-drink boxes, and enamel utensils scabbed and abscessed with wear, and old watches and cogs from machinery, and knives and forks—all of it was beautiful, she said, and she put it away in case she found a way of combining the things into a work of art.

She ran warm water into a plastic tub and put out her arms for Mahalia.

"I'll bathe her, if you like," she said.

"No," said Matt, "I'll do it. She's *my* baby, all right?" His vehemence startled Mahalia, and she started to cry, angry with the sudden tension she sensed in his body.

His greatest fear was that his mother would take over, that he'd *let* her take over.

But bathing Mahalia relaxed him again; he soaped her body all over till she was as slippery as an eel and rinsed her off. He swaddled her firmly in a towel and kissed her lightly on the forehead. She peered up at him, her face serious and wise.

The thing Mahalia would want to know one day would be *why*. And then *how*.

The *how* would be easier. That was the birds and the bees stuff. His own mother had always been frank about that since he was very young. He thought he could cope with that. The *why* would be harder to explain. Why he and Emmy had had her.

Mahalia was starting to play with sounds. Today she'd gone *mum mum mum mum mum*, and he'd echoed her back. Before too long he'd be able to talk to her properly, and tell her things.

If he were to explain why she had come into existence, he supposed he could put it down to all those days when he and Emmy should have been at school spent lying on the riverbank, watching the clouds. He could put her down to clouds. Or to beetles lumbering through the grass, the way Emmy's eyes lit up when she put one down his back so that he just had to tickle her.

For that was where it had started, their delight in each other, and one thing leading to another.

* * *

7

Mahalia

Emmy was the most reckless person he'd ever met. When Matt was with her, nothing was ordinary. He was in an *other* world: an Emmy world. The other-worldliness surrounded her, and enveloped him as well. It was a world that existed behind the dimension of ordinary life.

She had a way of making everything special. There was a sort of magic attached to her. And, magically, she had a way of getting what she wanted.

She said that for ages she'd had this thing about climbing the bell tower of the Catholic cathedral in Lismore. It was a square squat tower with a round turret attached to the side. "I bet nuns live there," she said. "With their noses in a prayer book. Shut up in there all the time to pray."

Matt was shocked. Emmy was a good Catholic girl. They hadn't yet begun missing school to lie about on the riverbank together.

"I'm going to climb that tower," she told him. "I've been wanting to since I was a kid."

She dragged him to the church office and put on her most demure Catholic-girl demeanor. She told the priest how she'd been wanting to climb the tower all her life, and now she felt she was old enough and responsible enough. She said nothing of her wild and insulting fantasies about nuns.

The priest was reluctant to allow them up the tower. He talked about the danger. Proper channels and so on. "But I thought you were the proper channel," she said, eyes downcast.

Matt squirmed and wished for invisibility. He watched a fly on the wall take off and exit through the open door. Emmy's conversation with the priest became a buzz in his head and he prepared to be shown the door. He prepared to follow the fly, ignominiously.

And then the priest took some keys from a drawer, and they followed the tramp of his no-nonsense black polished shoes through a back entrance to the cathedral, into the polished-wood stained-glass hush, where light entered as though from behind clouds. And there was the door that led to the tower.

The priest unlocked the door and threw a light switch. The bells were controlled by computer; he warned against staying in the bell room at the times when they would ring, and told them not to climb the ladders onto the roof.

Emmy promised they wouldn't.

Then, as soon as the priest departed, she grabbed Matt's hand and dragged him up the spiral staircase. It was all rough brick-work and narrow, impossible windows. They reached the first floor of the tower—a dim room, empty except for dust and a wooden lectern, lit only by a small stained-glass window. Emmy was disappointed. No nuns shut up with their prayer books.

She grabbed Matt and kissed him for the first time. In that room where she'd hoped for nuns. Her mouth tasted of pink lollipops. Her tongue was muscular and inquisitive.

They kissed again in the room on the next floor too, where the bell handles were arrayed in rows and numbered. Cardboard sheets were scattered on the floor, with words and numbers to show which bells were to be rung. *Silent night, Holy night:* 11 6 11 5 3 12.

The second kiss was quicker. Just when he was beginning to enjoy it, just when he was becoming familiar with her tongue, and felt that the taste of pink lollipops was the center of his world, Emmy pulled away. She led him up the next short section of stairs to the bells. They were tilted on their sides, twelve of them, different sizes; their clappers were still, waiting to be released—a dozen silenced metal tongues.

The light was bright up there, for this was the top of the tower, open on all sides to allow the sound to ring out. Matt could see the town outside: the houses up on the hill and sporting fields and clumps of camphor-laurel trees. He and Emmy put their faces into the wind and held them there for a long time. The air was like lemon soda water, and Matt wanted to drink and drink.

A green ladder led to a walkway above the bells. From that walkway was another ladder to a trapdoor out onto the roof, which Emmy had promised the priest she wouldn't climb.

Emmy's face was full of mischief and possibility. "I did promise," she said, demurely and unconvincingly.

"But I want to," she added.

For Emmy, wanting to do something and doing it followed each other naturally and inevitably. Matt went with her out of fear. Fear of being without her; fear of what she would say. Because, already, he would do anything for her.

He helped push open the trapdoor to the roof. And stood leaning over the parapet with her. "Someone will see," he heard himself say, feeling ashamed of his craving for conventionality.

Someone will see, he thought as she kissed him for the third time, the wind whipping their hair, in full view, he imagined, of the whole of Lismore.

"Don't be silly. No one ever looks up here. No one cares about this tower. Only me, and I'm up here, aren't I?"

His mother's house was a patchwork, made up of bits and pieces: odd items of timber, doors, windows—more doors and windows than any house needed, collected from secondhand building yards. Despite the surfeit of doors elsewhere—doors that led nowhere, just plugged a gap in the wall—the living room opened straight out onto the veranda with no door at all, just a wide gap. When it was rainy or cold, Matt had to shut the door of his room to stop the draft blowing in. From the outside, the house looked like a collection of old windows and doors that someone had left in a pile to see if it could rearrange itself into the semblance of a house of its own accord, and somehow it had. Somehow it all worked.

Matt felt that his life was like that. In optimistic moments he felt that he and Mahalia had all the bits there and somehow they'd make something of it one way or another, even if it did get a bit drafty sometimes.

And at other times he wasn't so sure.

Matt had left school a year ago. There was never a time that he remembered liking it, not even in kindergarten.

Mahalia

Not that he wasn't smart. Growing up in the bush in the house that his mother had cobbled together from odds and ends, he knew the names of all the birds that came to the garden by the age of four, those of a dozen rainforest plants at five; he could read then too, and write *Tyrannosaurus* and sort the shells they'd collected at the beach into their different types. At six he went to school and learned how profoundly boring it could be.

He met Emmy at the age of fifteen, and they became a team, sneaking off from school together to spend the day lying on the riverbank, or hitching over to the beach at Byron Bay. They loved the way the long stretch of beach was different every single time, the way the color of the water changed with changes in the sky, and they always found shells and strange bits and pieces the sea had thrown up. Matt put them in his pockets and they started their own collection of beach treasures, each of them a memento of a particular day. Emmy said you should never let a day pass unnoticed, that it should be memorable and particular and special. She said it was a *sin* to let time pass unheeded and unregarded, to *waste* it like that.

After Matt left school, Social Security sent him to countless courses designed to give him life skills and *build his self-esteem*, but what he wanted was a job of the kind that didn't exist anymore: a job where you didn't need any book learning and where you could get by on good honest toil.

He planted trees in reforestation projects and helped stabilize riverbanks, but all that was left at the end of these short-term jobs was welfare—again.

When Emmy left, he had to declare on his form that he had

separated from his partner. And he found himself on the single supporting parent's pension.

There was the inevitable interview with the social worker; hours spent with Mahalia strapped in her possum pouch on his chest while he waited to be dealt with. He paced and rocked her, murmuring soft words. He watched numbers flash onto a screen and checked them against his docket. His head screamed at the mindless daytime TV; the monitor was placed on a bracket up near the ceiling so that no one could get away from it. He sat in one of the detestable gray plastic chairs and stared at the gray walls, and somehow his feelings transferred themselves to Mahalia, for she stiffened her body and screamed and screamed under the fluorescent lights.

Finally it was all over. He had said all the right things, and he had smiled (he couldn't help himself; it was part of his nature to smile). He said his mother could help him with the baby. But all the time he felt sure he didn't need help, just the money necessary for them to stay alive. In the end that was all that was forthcoming anyway.

Matt's mother had the bluest of eyes, and still wore her hair long, adding henna to soften the appearance of white strands in the black. One of her friends trimmed it for her. "Now that you're forty, maybe you should think of cutting it short."

His mother looked stricken. "I will one day. But not yet. Not yet."

Her hair was her only vanity. She wore no makeup, and dressed always in shorts or jeans and men's shirts she bought at thrift shops. Even at work she got away with a tidy variation of her *uniform*, as she called it.

She said that lipstick *rotted your brain*.

If she wasn't wearing her gumboots, they were on the back veranda, caked in mud. Her fingernails were often filthy with earth from gardening, or oil from the engine of her van. She slashed lantana and planted trees and vegetables.

She and Matt had been alone all their lives. His father hadn't wanted children, so she'd brought Matt up by herself, with no contact, really, no support. "Though I wouldn't have minded if he'd wanted to take part in you," she'd said. She made it sound like a bushwalk she'd invited someone to.

Matt had felt the loss. It was such a lonely house, with just the two of them, even though his mother had filled it with music and flowers and the beautiful things she made. Matt had missed the ordinariness of daily contact with a father. He determined when he was very young that he would see his own children grow up.

His mother had done everything she could to see that he didn't miss out. She took him to parks and taught him to kick a soccer ball around. He remembered her running and running, her black hair flying out behind her, leaping and kicking at the ball, her legs in long red-and-green football socks. She brought home books on paper airplanes, and they sat at the kitchen table together, folding and experimenting. Matt had the best paper airplanes of any kid he knew.

There were friends, lots of friends, and people who stayed with them for extended periods. There were men who stayed the night in his mother's bedroom sometimes, but none had been allowed to share their life. There were men who were *just friends*. One of them, Peter, had taught him to play the guitar. But as far as Matt could see, these men weren't much different from his mother: they struggled with cantankerous vehicles and slashed and planted and watered in their spare time. They always had half-completed houses with many pairs of muddy gumboots on the veranda.

When Emmy and Matt knew they were going to have a baby, they went to her parents and told them they intended to keep it.

Keep Mahalia, as it turned out.

Emmy's parents as good as told them they were crazy. Evil, even, to consider it. Which Matt supposed was why Emmy wouldn't have anything to do with them, afterward.

"But what can you offer a baby?" they said. "You have no job, no money, no prospects, nothing. You're too young. You really should think about what you're doing. You can have it adopted. There are thousands of couples who could give a baby a good home."

"But we want it," Emmy told them, "and it's ours, and we'll love it, and that's more than a lot of babies have. We'll give it love.

"We'll just love it, okay?"

When Emmy had first gone away, Matt had watched anxiously for a sign that Mahalia sensed it. But he'd been so numb himself that he couldn't be sure. Now, at his mother's place, he still felt subdued and watchful. He listened to the sound of the rain on the roof and felt that the world was muffled and enveloped by it.

His mother stood on the veranda for a long time. Earlier, just before nightfall, she'd waited for the first bats to come flying out of the forest, watching them stream in a thickening dark cloud toward the horizon on their nightly quest for food. Every now and then one would turn back and fly against the tide, and then just as suddenly resume the forward journey. The sight of her watching their vigorous hopeful flight saddened Matt; he thought she brooded too much about the world. Leaning on the rail, she stared out at mist and cloud. She held her hand, palm up, out to receive the rain.

When Matt was much younger and he saw her sad like that, he would put his arms around her and kiss her, and that always made her happy again. Now he stood awkwardly on the veranda in the pale light from the living room with Mahalia in his arms. He said, "D'you want to come and kiss her good night? We're going to bed now."

That night Matt slept beside Mahalia in his childhood bed, a bed full of comforts and memories. His mother had come in to kiss Mahalia good night, and he remembered how, even quite recently, when he was about fourteen or fifteen, she used to come and sit on the edge of his bed and chat before he went to sleep— not about heavy stuff, just about what they'd both been doing during the day, and funny stuff, like the time a young kookaburra had crashed into one of the windows and nearly knocked itself out, and how *embarrassed* it had looked while it sat there recovering before it flew away.

But tonight his mother had stood uncertainly in the doorway of the room before going, looking as if she wanted to say something only she wasn't sure what, and it was she who'd looked embarrassed.

Matt put Mahalia next to the wall so that she couldn't fall out.

He missed Emmy beside him at night, the way she curled into the shape of his sleeping back. He longed for the earthy smell of her hair when he woke next to her in the morning. His whole body hurt with missing her, and that was something new to him. He hadn't known that the lack of someone could be felt like a real, physical ache.

Mahalia slept like someone gathering strength to get on with her life. Her fists were bunched up beside her face, her eyes tightly closed. It was sleep with purpose.

Matt lay awake, staring into the dark for a long time, his hands behind his head. Outside, it still rained lightly, sounding like whispers on the iron roof. He knew that someone else in his situation—a young man with his life ahead of him—would leave the baby with his mother. But he wanted Mahalia. He had always wanted her. He felt that he'd wanted her even before he had known of the possibility of her. There was nothing else to do but to care for her; he had helped look after her from the start anyway. But it was different on your own. Already he felt the lack of someone to turn to, to say *Should we* . . . or *Perhaps* . . .

Matt was the one who was always thinking about how they should care for her. Emmy, who used to be so decisive, would always say vaguely, "If you like . . . ," or "I don't mind . . . ," so he ended up making the decisions, even about stupid little things, like buying cream to put on the rash on Mahalia's bottom, or giving her extra water in a bottle on a hot day.

Matt slept at last. Like Mahalia, he needed to gather strength to get on with his life. She woke in the night, as she always did, and he switched on a light and stumbled out to warm a bottle. He held her in his arms and fed her in the dark, propped up in the warm bed; her eyes were dark in the night, and she sucked with the same intensity that she put into everything. When Mahalia was newborn, she had looked as helpless as a squirming kitten, and Emmy had whispered to him, "I never want anything to harm her. I feel so scared for her."

But Mahalia had a tenacious capacity for life; she fed and grew and learned. When Matt was alone with her in the dead of night like this, he felt a great surge of feeling for her. *We're in this together*, her serious gaze told him, and he was grateful that she was in his life. Whatever happened, he didn't want to wish her away.

Mahalia stopped sucking and he knew she'd fallen asleep again. He pulled the bottle gently from her mouth, wiped a drop of milk from her chin, and snuggled her down beside him. A gum tree stroked its branch across the window. A wind had come up, and it sighed through the trees. His room, which he'd had since he was a child and was still full of his childish stuff, smelled of baby now, sweet and milky, a soft skin smell.

The next morning Matt woke bleary-eyed to find Mahalia beside him, cooing, on her stomach for the first time. "So," he said, "you can roll over, can you? I'll have to be sure you can't roll off a bed from now on."

He changed her diaper, and she immediately rolled onto her stomach again, lifting up her neck from the bed and kicking her legs like a swimmer.

"Clever Mahalia," he said. "Clever, clever Mahalia."

It rained for two weeks.

Mahalia noticed the rain, he was sure. She lay in her crib in the mornings and listened to it falling on the roof, babbling to it. "Goo," Matt said to her. "Ka," she replied. He picked her up and went out onto the veranda, and she blinked and looked at the stream of water falling over the edge of the roof. She could turn her head now and look at things she wanted to see.

"It's bloody wet, that's what it is, Mahalia," he said. "Still, better get used to it, this is what the weather's like in this neck of the woods." He liked using phrases like *neck of the woods*. They made him feel connected to the old times. Matt liked old blokes; he liked sitting and having a yarn with them. *Having a yarn*. That was another phrase they used. And *grub*, and *tucker*. All good words. Old words.

Mahalia coughed. It wasn't a real cough, just the cough she'd discovered she could use to attract Matt's attention. Not that she needed it at this moment.

"You're a little bullshit artist," he said, and tickled her under her arms. She laughed and squealed, and jerked her body away from him so suddenly that he almost dropped her.

Mahalia

"How about a bath?" he said. "I know it's wet outside, but you stink."

Matt sat Mahalia on the floor, where she could hold herself upright by leaning forward and resting her weight on her hands. He gave her a plastic cup to look at, and she picked it up with one hand and put it to her mouth experimentally. He warmed some water on the stove and tipped it into her bath, testing the temperature with his elbow.

Mahalia loved a bath. She had learned that she could splash the water with the palm of her hand; it made her squeal with excitement and delight. She played with the soap and squelched it through her fingers.

When the bath was over, Matt toweled her, dusted her with powder, and dressed her in a clean jumpsuit.

"There you go—good as new."

She loved to crumple paper, so he sat her on the floor and handed her the one-page letter he'd written to Emmy. Mahalia crushed it and put it to her mouth and slobbered over it, as he'd known she would. It was one way of solving the problem of what to do with the letter. He couldn't seem to find the right words.

On Mahalia's second day of life, when they were alone with her, Emmy and Matt unwrapped their baby from the sheet that swaddled her tightly and removed her clothes in order to look at her properly. They had both seen her when she was born, of course, but that had been a time when they were dazed and exhausted and unable to take in the miracle of her.

Unwrapped, she became a squalling, red-faced bundle of jerking limbs. Her feet were tiny and wrinkled and untried against the earth. Matt cupped her face with his large, tender, wondering hands and massaged the side of her face gently till she stopped crying. He lifted her up and cradled her against his chest.

"Your mother came," said Emmy. "Thank goodness she didn't go on like all the relatives visiting in the hospital. 'Oh, who do you think he looks like? He's got Uncle Stan's nose, and Auntie Vera's chin!'" Matt knew she was hiding her disappointment that his mother had been the only relative to visit.

"What did she say?" asked Matt.

"She said that she's beautiful. And that we'll be all right," said Emmy, nodding in a satisfied way. Watching Matt with her, she'd said shyly, "I wonder what she'll think of her father's music?"

Matt remembered this as he sat in his mother's house listening to the rain and playing his guitar. It was an electric bass guitar, and played without amplification, the strings made a deep resonant rhythm that Mahalia liked. He sat her on the floor in front of him and she grabbed hold of her feet and made sounds of her own to accompany his music.

One day the sky cleared and Matt took the opportunity to get out of the house, leaving Mahalia with his mother. He strode up the road, feeling pleasure in being able to stretch his legs with vigorous exercise, get some air into his lungs. It was the first time in ages he'd been anywhere without Mahalia strapped to him, and at first he reveled in the freedom. But the road was long and tedious, with no outlook, only endless forest, and there came a point where he'd had enough, and he hurried back to see Mahalia, feeling the absence of her now as a loss.

The house was empty when he returned, but the radio was

playing, and guessing where his mother might be, he went at once to the place at the edge of the garden where she'd worn a narrow path into the rainforest. It was her own private, secret track, almost invisible. The wait-a-while vine whipped out long, jagged strands and caught at his clothing, sticking like Velcro. Extricating himself, he needed to push through the forest for only a few minutes till he came to the fig tree.

His mother was leaning against it, with Mahalia strapped to her front in the carry pouch. It was a tree that had a trunk like a human torso, muscled, stretching up through the canopy, where its branch arms reached out into the light. It was the archetypal rainforest tree, the stuff of calendars and postcards but no less remarkable for that.

She looked round as he approached her, and smiled. Without speaking, they started to walk out of the forest together, their footsteps padding on the damp leaves and crackling the occasional vine.

Matt had once overheard her saying to a friend, "Any kid worth its salt rebels against its parents sometimes," and he wondered now if he had rebelled. Only by having Mahalia so young . . . Otherwise, he'd felt the burden of being the only child of a single parent. When she was feeling sad, he was the only one there to cheer her up. Once, she had sat with her cheek on her hand at the kitchen table, silent and thoughtful and seemingly unreachable. He'd crept to their newly made composting toilet, one in which tiger worms ate everything they put into it. Pulling out the tray at the back, he discovered the first lovely, silty remains of their castings.

He took it to her in the lid of a jam jar and pushed it shyly across the table toward her. "Look," he said, "what our poo has turned into."

She smiled at him: a real, happy smile.

"Smell it," urged Matt. "It's so clean and sweet."

She lifted the lid to her nose. "Lovely!" she agreed. And with a burst of optimism, she'd got up and made a pot of tea for herself and an orange juice for him, clattering happily in the kitchen, and they'd sat together sipping their drinks with the lid full of rich black compost in a place of honor at the center of the table.

Matt wished that Mahalia could see the view. Even through rain, it amazed him.

The blue of those hills always knocked him out, though it was a sight he'd seen for the whole of his life. And clouds. How could you describe clouds? The way the sun hit them and lit them up, the *shapes* they formed into, a particular kind on a certain day, as if the universe had woken up that morning and said, *I think I'll make me a whole lot of high wispy ones today, all identical.* And having done that one day, it showed off and made even more amazing ones the next.

The view was unbelievable, holy almost.

In the house, though, everything was ordinary, claustrophobic, especially in the wet. If he didn't have that view outside, he'd go mad.

Mahalia smiled at the sound of his voice. When she was fussing about something, it was enough to soothe her.

She talked to him. They held conversations, of a kind, one of them making a sound and the other responding. Mahalia put more meaning into a gurgle than other people put into an entire sentence.

23

But she could frustrate him. Sometimes he had to struggle to put her diaper on. One day she kept evading him, rolling over gleefully every time at the exact moment when he was about to plunge the pin into the cloth. And she was strong; he felt her pit her strength against his, and knew that this was only the beginning of her testing him out.

"Shit, Mahalia, keep *still*!" he said, wrenching her over onto her back so forcefully that she cried out. He shoved the pin in angrily, blindly, and it connected with the flesh of her stomach. There was silence while she registered the unexpected pain with an intake of breath so deep and sustained that he thought for one heart-pounding moment that she'd stopped breathing.

Then came the outraged bellow, and his relief was so great that his anger reignited. "Now look what you've made me do!"

He was shocked to hear himself speak to his own baby that way. She lay on the floor, crying at the unexpected pain the world could inflict on her. Gently, gingerly, he put the pin in place. He picked Mahalia up and hugged her against his shoulder. "I didn't mean it, Mahalia, baby," he said. "I didn't mean it."

When Mahalia was first born, it had been sheer wonder waking to her each day. Every part of her was a miracle, and when she woke at night, he was immediately at her side, soothing her and gazing at the impossibility of her tiny fingers and toes, her astonishment of spiky black hair (which she entirely lost soon afterward). They waited to name her, waiting to see what name attached itself to her, until finally, when she'd been in the world a week, Matt said shyly to Emmy, "I think Mahalia would be a nice name."

"Mahalia," she said. "That's unusual. I've never even heard it before."

"She was a singer. A gospel singer. One of the best."

And Emmy had agreed. Still sleepy and sore and milky, she said, "Okay. If you like."

Now there was always the routine. *Change Mahalia, feed Mahalia, keep Mahalia clean, wash the diapers, clean the bottles, boil the water for the formula.*

Mahalia started to teethe, crying angrily, and gnawing on her fists. She kept Matt awake at night with her wails, but he held her and sang to her in his tuneless voice till she slept. He gave her hard things to chew on, bits of celery and crusts of bread, and she gnawed on them with desperation. Finally they were through, two sharp white buds in her lower jaw.

Matt found that you could spend all day playing with a baby. Mahalia laughed and chortled with excitement when their play got wild, but Matt was astonished how quickly her squeals of delight could turn into an annoyed scream.

His mother loved to be with her. She sat and played with Mahalia for ages when she had time, and Mahalia showed her grandmother how strong she was becoming: when she was held up, she could bounce up and down and take her weight on her legs.

A friend dropped in: Elijah, who'd left school the same time as Matt, but hadn't burdened himself with a baby. He hadn't found a job either, but drifted from friend to friend, staying for days at a time sometimes. He lived at home the rest of the time.

Mahalia

Matt had tried to write a song about Elijah once, but all he came up with was a list of stuff that described Elijah, and he could never fit any of it together so that it satisfied him.

The list went:

He
    has a skinny wiry crafty body
He
    has eyes that dart about, missing nothing
He
    is always nervously moving,
    always off to somewhere
He
    wants to be the hero of his own story
    only he isn't sure what it is yet
He
    always says *What a hero!*
    when someone is being tough
    not really meaning it
He
    is short
    but acts tall
He
    is tough in his own way
    but tender in a way that he'll never let other people
    know about
He
    is too soft for his own good

When he gave up trying to finish the song, Matt just plinked along on his guitar, thinking of the notes as words that he couldn't quite find.

Matt was ashamed of the way that he and Emmy were so exclusive after they got together. They were a little band of two. Matt had neglected Elijah. But now Elijah had come to see him, and Matt was grateful.

Elijah was full of plans. "Think I'll go up to Stanthorpe, do some apple picking," he said. "Get myself some money together to buy a car. Then I'll be set! Get about all over the place, go where I like. Buy a wagon, live in the back of it. I'll get a dog too; a dog's the best friend in the world. Hey, you could come too. Leave the baby with ya mum, she'll look after it. A few months' picking, you could set yourself up."

Matt didn't answer. "Hey, look at this!" he said as Mahalia rolled from her back onto her front and pushed the front of her body up with her arms. "I reckon she'll be crawling soon. You're a regular little athlete, you are," he told her. "Hey, mate, look! She's got teeth!" Matt showed Elijah Mahalia's latest achievement. "They're as serrated as steak knives!"

Matt strapped Mahalia to his chest and they wandered down to the creek, just as they used to do, Elijah raving and waving his arms, his dark eyes darting to Matt's face to suss out what he was thinking about.

They sat on a rock, and Elijah fished in his pocket for the makings of a durry. Matt hadn't smoked for a long time, but he took a few puffs to be sociable, making sure he blew the smoke away from Mahalia. When he felt mildly stoned, he waved the rest of the joint away. He had to stay on top of things.

"You do much fishing these days?"

Matt shook his head.

"Hey, you know what makes good bait? Get a green tree frog, wrap 'im in a bit of paperbark, and roast 'im."

"Yeah?" said Matt. Inside, he was cracking up. "Anyway, aren't they protected or something?"

Elijah was always full of bush wisdom. Matt used to admire that once, used to listen to him. Once they'd made a bark hut together and stayed in it a couple of nights in the bush, but that was years ago, before Matt had shut him out.

"What happened with Emmy?" said Elijah softly and cannily and out of the blue. "She piss off on ya?"

"Yeah, mate," said Matt, still laughing inside about the tree frog. He didn't mind Elijah's question, or the way he put it. It was just his way. "Well," he said, "she got a bit unhappy and confused. She's sorting herself out."

Elijah nodded. "Anyway, I reckon you're a saint, looking after the kid."

Matt shook his head. "No, I'm not. I *want* to look after her. Anyway, I'm no saint. I get really angry and pissed off with her sometimes." He remembered the time he'd jabbed the diaper pin into her. Mahalia was at this moment behaving like an angel, sitting on his knee watching the sparkle on the surface of the water. He bent down and kissed the top of her head, smelling the distinctive, sweet odor of her scalp. He'd heard somewhere that sniffing the top of a baby's head could make you feel high, that you could get addicted to it.

On the way back, Elijah found a tick on the back of his neck and pulled it out and ate it. "Makes you immune to 'em," he said. "Or so they reckon."

"Yeah, well, I don't think I'll try it," said Matt, laughing.

Elijah left soon after they got back, to drop in on someone else he knew. Matt was thankful he hadn't wanted to stay. It was good to see Elijah, but there was a gulf there as well.

You're getting too serious, Matt told himself when Elijah had gone. *Thinking about babies all the time. No wonder your old friends don't want to talk to you.*

4

The only friend Matt hadn't drifted away from was Otis, and Matt visited him and his family often. It was easygoing. They were easy people to be with. *Family* to them meant a shifting population of relatives, and Matt and Mahalia were accepted as just another couple of people around the house. No one asked nosy questions about where Emmy had gone, or why. They considered that wasn't their business. If Emmy had gone away, well, then she would come again, perhaps. They were people of few words, and at that time Matt didn't want words or explanations, just laughter, music, and acceptance.

Otis planned to be a teacher. Otis's father, Alan, thought he should be a blues guitarist. The guitar was Otis's passion, but he wanted a real job. They bickered about it in a good-natured way.

"Let 'im be a teacher!" said his auntie Charmian, gesturing magnanimously with a marshmallow cookie.

"That's not on your diabetes diet, Charm," said Alan sternly. He was Charmian's brother; she lived with them most of the time, when she wasn't off down south visiting relatives or staying with her daughter and her family nearby. She was like a mother to Otis because his own mother had died when he was little.

"This? It's just a little cookie. Not much sugar in this." Charmian's voice lilted on the words *little cookie*, making it sound completely innocent. Her round brown face and sleepy eyes caught Matt's glance and she raised her eyebrows in a good-humored gesture that said *How do I put up with him?* She always said that Alan was a big tease.

Matt wished he had a father who wanted him to be a blues guitarist. Alan was so certain of Otis's ability and talent; he didn't care, as Otis always told him, that most musicians struggled for years to make a living. *But you'll make it in the end*, he always said, and *Who cares about money?* Matt noticed him watching Otis play sometimes with such a look of sweet loving longing on his face that Matt felt envious.

Alan was a handsome man, with a strong jaw, a long hooked nose, and flashing eyes. He was fit and young-looking; he made sure he jogged every day and he kicked a ball around the field with Otis and his mates when he could. Yet he'd rarely had a job; no one employed Kooris in country towns except the government.

Teaching would suck, Matt thought, but Otis worked hard at school. He had goals, something Matt had never had. Otis's ordinary, stolid, pudgy face, what Americans would call *homely*, was as familiar to Matt as his own. *An ugly black bastard* was how Otis had once described himself, his voice light and quick and care-less, lifting his eyebrows to show he didn't give a shit what he looked like.

As he tried out a few chords on his guitar, he leaned over it in a way that was both tender and modest. "Hey, Matt, listen to this," he said. "I got this off that Muddy Waters record I picked up the other day."

Mahalia

Charmian strode across the room to where Mahalia sat patiently on the floor, looking up in awe at all the big people in the room. Charmian moved majestically, like a sailing boat. She made plumpness a graceful asset. "How's my beautiful baby *girl?*" she said. She picked Mahalia up. "My God, this kid's heavy. She grown like crazy since you was here before. What you been feeding her on, Matt?"

Mahalia put her hand experimentally into Charmian's mouth, and Charmian nibbled on her fingers for a moment. "I could eat you up!" she told Mahalia.

Matt and Otis tuned their guitars. Even when Matt had been so exclusively with Emmy, he'd found time to see Otis occasionally, their music the glue that kept them together. The other friends Matt used to have all liked partying too much, and with a baby to care for, he didn't go to parties anymore; he didn't drink and hang out like they did, with one day sliding over into another unnoticed and unregarded. He had Mahalia to look after, and the routine of caring for her was his life now. *Millstone*, he sometimes whispered to her, *Ball and chain*. He didn't know whether he meant it or not. He didn't know whether he minded, not yet, for it was all still so new, and difficult, and he knew that he had no choice.

"I love this baby!" said Charmian, with a wicked look toward Matt. She was a *big tease* too. "Can I keep 'er?"

Matt smiled and plugged his guitar into Otis's amp. He strummed a few notes, his ear cocked to the vibrations of the instrument. He loved the thick bass notes it produced, like a drumbeat almost. A lot of guitarists found playing bass boring, but not Matt. He could even practice without playing along to a record, enjoying the steady thunk of the strings and getting right into the rhythm of it.

Otis's face transformed itself when he played. It responded to the music he pulled from the guitar, each note affecting the muscles of his face: one made him wince in pain, the next softened and relaxed him. The sound affected his body: this note made his shoulder twitch, that one caused his elbow to squeeze against the side of his body, with the next his back hunched over. Matt was absolutely motionless when he played, his fingers the only part of his body that moved. His rhythm provided the steady brown thread that Otis's notes wove around and through, fizzing with color, soaring and warbling like a bird, then squeaking like a bat.

"Man, that was beautiful," said Matt when they'd finished.

"Yeah!" said Alan, interjecting from the next room. "And he tells me he wants to be a teacher!"

Matt dreamed in blue. He dreamed the blue of the room in his father's house, and he dreamed the blue of the Mediterranean Sea, which he'd never seen but only heard of. He dreamed of the blues, which he and Otis played together, and the blue of his mother's eyes.

He woke, and lay and watched Mahalia as she surfaced from sleep. She cooed to herself, gazing at the shadows that danced on the walls. Kicking off her bedclothes, she caught hold of her toes and stared at the mobile of fish that her grandmother had made for her, watching as they swam through the early-morning light. She reached out to touch the light but it escaped through her fingers.

The light had seeped into Matt's dreams, dreams of distance and warm blue sea. He'd woken with the blue still with him and he'd thought that it would be a good day to take Mahalia to the beach. It was spring.

He got a lift into town with his mother when she went to work. He needed to get Mahalia a hat. At St. Vinnie's, Matt found several cotton hats for babies and tried them on her. As each hat went on her head, she reached up, pulled it off, and dropped it on the floor.

"You'll have to find one that ties under the chin."

Matt saw the girl who spoke as beautiful, though many would have found her ugly. Her long tawny hair curled around her head in a mane, and her eyes were just a bit too close together and somehow centered on her nose, so that, with the hair, her face was altogether like a lion's: questioning and clever and sure of itself.

Matt had noticed her earlier, but now, embarrassed that she might have seen him watching her out of the corner of his eye, he could barely look at her. She'd been trying on an assortment of clothes in front of a mirror, and had not needed to go into a dressing room because she'd merely put the clothes on over whatever she was already wearing, so that there was layer upon layer. But she'd shown a noticeable quantity of leg and bare brown midriff: she managed to combine black stretch leggings, a short purple silk skirt, a white net petticoat like a ballet tutu, a pink tank top over a green T-shirt, and a silver cardigan embroidered with rosebuds.

She tugged off the cardigan and the net petticoat and knelt down beside Mahalia's stroller. "Don't you want to wear a hat? The sun will burn you if you don't." She looked into Mahalia's face as she spoke.

She got up and rummaged in the baby clothes for another hat. Mahalia merely stared at her with round-eyed dumb awe as the girl placed a terry-cloth hat on her head and tied it under the chin with strings. Mahalia put her hand to the crown of her head, touched the hat, and brought her hand down again, a look of wonder on her face.

"That's a *good* hat. A *very* good hat," the lion girl told Mahalia firmly, smiling at her so cheerfully that Mahalia smiled back, despite her dubious feeling about the thing that had been placed on her head.

"See?" said the girl to Matt. "Isn't that just what you're after? I'm an ace thrift shopper. Call on me anytime."

She flashed him the smile that had charmed Mahalia, a smile that had as much to do with a sudden upward glance full of humor as it did with teeth and mouth. Then she backed away a couple of steps, almost bashfully, and turned sharply and walked to the counter. Matt was left with an impression of bare brown feet and a lion's mane and a smile that reminded him acutely, and painfully, of Emmy.

On the way out of town to hitch to the beach, Matt stopped at the health-food shop for some carob buttons. He looked at the notices on the board and found one that interested him:

LARGE ROOM WITH BALCONY IN SHOPFRONT HOUSE
FRIENDLY HOUSEHOLD, VEGGIE GARDEN, CHILD WELCOME
OPTIONAL FREE SINGING LESSONS INCLUDED

Matt tore the address (SORRY, NO PHONE, it said) from the strip at the bottom and put it in his pocket, and made his way out to the main coast road to hitch.

Mahalia

The wheels of Mahalia's stroller sang along the concrete paths of Lismore; they rasped and whirred across the blue metal roads, whisking right past the used-car lots, where Matt had spent too many boring hours in his youth with Elijah, who drooled over what he called the *beasts*. And the crappy wooden houses of Lismore leered and beckoned, for Matt had known many a person who lived in them; the flat he and Emmy had shared before she went away was up that street there. And high above the old part of Lismore, the part that flooded, with its three bridges crossing its two rivers, and its pubs and clubs and the most deadly boring main street in the entire universe, nestled the houses of the newer suburbs, the houses with trim gardens and views. Emmy's parents lived up there, watching television and vacuuming the wall-to-wall carpet and washing up three times a day. And there was the cathedral, with the squat date palm and the tower that he and Emmy had climbed, and there were the camphor-laurel trees they had seen from the tower, and here was the road that led out of town, and here was a van stopping for him.

He arrived at the beach that day with a joyful heart, despite (or perhaps because of) the smile of the girl in the thrift shop that had reminded him of how much he was missing Emmy. Emmy had a way of looking at him, of lifting the corners of her mouth and lighting up her eyes somehow at the same time, so that her whole face was surprised and joyful. She made him feel that he was the only person in the world she ever looked at like that. "Hey!" she'd say to him, grabbing an apple from the fruit bowl, her face alight with mischief. "Catch!"

Down on the sand he took Mahalia's diaper off and carried her down to the water. The hat the girl had found for her shaded her stern little face. She was solemnly aware that a new experience was happening to her and she was ready for it. He dipped her toes in the water and she curled up her feet and wrinkled her face and exclaimed. Then, when she was used to the feel of the cool water, he held her under the arms and bounced her up and down at the edge of the sea, and she flexed her legs and took her weight on her feet, digging her toes into sand for the first time in her life.

Matt was careful of her pale defenseless skin, and had left her shirt on, and after a short time he bundled her up in a towel and carried her back up into the shade. Then they walked down the beach to search for shells.

Reality, he told Mahalia, *is that nothing happens*. But he looked out at the sea, squinting at the curve of the coast from the lighthouse to where it disappeared into infinity in the north, and was quite content, at the moment, for nothing to happen.

He and Emmy had been on this beach once, with sand stretching forever, no one much around apart from strolling couples and a lone person doing yoga on the sand near the sea.

And there came a horse from behind them, a horse with a rider crouched low, and as it got closer, they saw it was a man with a bare chest, riding bareback and wearing a long feathered Indian headdress.

He swerved to avoid the walking couples and the yoga person, who didn't budge, and as he thundered past, Matt saw his face, bright with war paint, mouth pulled into a grimace, teeth sharp as a fox's: it was like staring into a mask. As he went past, he looked down at them; it seemed to Matt that he looked particularly at

Emmy. But he shot past them in a moment, and all they could see was the rear of the horse, its speckled rump, its hooves kicking up sand.

He stopped a little way up the beach and led the horse into the water, and soon they caught up with him. He appeared ordinary off the horse, just a man with a painted face and funny headgear and a bare brown chest.

Emmy paused to stroke the horse, talking to it all the while, and the man asked her if she'd like to get on it.

Once she was up on the horse's back holding the reins, Emmy looked out over the sea with an expression on her face Matt had never seen before. Without a word she dug her heels into the horse's flanks and took off. Matt heard the sound of hooves and saw the sand kicked up in their wake, and stood helplessly, watching her go. The red Indian grinned. He didn't look at Matt at all. He was the sort of *dude* who thought it was cool that some girl had just taken off on his horse.

And just when Matt thought Emmy would never come back, just keep going along that infinite beach until she became a speck and disappeared, she wheeled the horse around and returned, and he watched her coming closer and closer, crouched low over the horse's back.

When she reined it in, she was so close that Matt could see the sweat glistening under her nose. The red Indian grabbed the reins, and she slid off.

Matt put his face into her hair. All he could smell was horse sweat, and Emmy sweat; she pushed him away after a moment, and looked up at the horse with love, her face bright with exertion.

5

"The Bluebird Café," said his mother as they pulled up. She was dropping him off at the address he'd torn from the advertisement.

"What?"

"This place used to be the Bluebird Café. Years ago. Oh, when you were only a bit older than Mahalia. It didn't last long. It was one of those early hippie cafés. Fresh orange juice and veggie burgers. I don't think I ever went there. But I always remembered the name."

The place was a double-storied shopfront, with a veranda. The shop windows had been painted over to stop people peering in, in ocher and aqua paint, with a design of an arch and latticework.

A man answered the door, a pale man with a long ponytail. He had the look of someone who spent a lot of time in record shops flicking through old records, a look of shy fanaticism. "Yes?" he said. He had a flat, expressionless voice.

"I've come about the room?" said Matt, shifting Mahalia to his other hip. She was too big for the pouch now, and her fold-up stroller sat beside him on the footpath.

"The room? Oh. Yeah." It took him a long time to register what Matt had said.

Mahalia

"Er—come in. My name's Dave."

Matt picked up the stroller and took it inside with him. "Mind if I just leave it inside here?"

"What? Oh, sure." There were people who simply didn't notice babies, or strollers, ever, and Dave was one of them. He hadn't even glanced at Mahalia, let alone said hello to her, as many people would have done. Was this the place that advertised *child welcome*?

Once Matt's eyes had become accustomed to the darkness, he saw that they were in a large empty room with a few cardboard boxes stacked up around the edges and two sagging sofas. A timber staircase at the side led to the second story.

"Yeah," said Dave. "Well, we never seem to use this room. There's only Eliza and me here now and we congregate in the kitchen or stay in our own rooms. But come up and see the room that's for rent."

Even in a ponytail, Dave's hair reached to his waist. Perhaps that's where all his energy was, for he barely used a muscle in his face, and he led Matt up the stairs with a walk so languid that he appeared to begrudge the effort required to move.

"This room's been vacant for a while. We didn't bother getting anyone in. The thing is, I'm moving in with my girlfriend as soon as I can get someone to replace me. So when I leave, there'll be another room vacant as well. Eliza and whoever rents this can decide whether they want a third person."

Matt stared at Dave's heels as he climbed the stairs. Mahalia was in his arms, and he put his nose near the top of her head. The sweet smell of her soft bald scalp masked the musty dark odor of the house.

Dave led him into a large front room that was filled with light. It was painted yellow. The walls had become grubby and it was bare except for a small cardboard box with scraps of cloth in it. Matt liked the room immediately.

"Gets a bit of noise from the street," said Dave, opening the door that led to the veranda.

Matt went out. It was a deep veranda, partly closed in by peeling latticework. "What do you think, Mahalia?" he said. "A veranda!"

In his imagination he had already moved in.

He looked up approvingly toward the roof, where a red nylon rope was suspended from the rafters. "With a washing line."

The front door downstairs slammed.

Dave had followed Matt out to the veranda. "That sounds like Eliza," he said.

There were energetic footsteps on the stairs. Then someone walked briskly around the top floor.

"Eliza! Come out to the veranda!" called Dave.

Footsteps came through the yellow room. Bold, striding footsteps on the bare boards. A face appeared, the face of the lion girl.

She grinned at Matt, but it was Mahalia she spoke to. "How was that hat, eh? Keep the sun off you all right?" She was one of the people who noticed babies.

"Do you know each other?" said Dave, but his voice was devoid of surprise or curiosity.

"Not really. But we've met. Kind of." Eliza's almost-crossed eyes met Matt's.

"I'm Matt," he said, holding out his hand.

"Eliza," she said. "And this is?" She looked at Mahalia with a quizzical look.

Mahalia

"Oh. This is Mahalia." Matt positioned her so she could see Eliza better.

"Wow! Mahalia! After Mahalia Jackson?"

"Yeah."

An awkward silence followed. She'd expected him to say more. Matt finally found his voice.

"Who gives the optional free singing lessons?"

"I do," said Eliza.

Eliza had given him a key, and there was no one home when he moved in. Matt noticed that his mother tactfully made no comment about the darkness and the sparse nature of the furnishings in the front room, the former shop, which was so obviously used as a kind of dumping ground for junk rather than a living room.

"Our room's up here."

He opened the door onto the veranda to let in some air, and his mother looked around.

"Needs a sweep," he said, anticipating her feelings about it.

"Oh, it's nice," she said warmly. "A good room. Big. Lots of light."

They set up Mahalia's crib first and put her in it while they moved Matt's things. (His mother had bought the crib second-hand and painted it mauve. "You think I can't buy my own grand-daughter a crib?" she'd said when Matt protested.) Mahalia sat on the bare mattress, rattling the bars, looking as if she might cry at any moment.

Matt squatted down to look at the box of things that had been left behind in the corner. There were some pieces of bright fabric and a few tubes of glitter.

"You want?" he asked his mother, showing the box and its contents to her. She nodded happily. It was exactly the kind of stuff she collected.

"Visit me!" she said sternly as she left him to settle in. He stood on the balcony and watched her car pull away. He thought of the emptiness of the house on the mountain that she was going back to. She loved the quiet, she had chosen it, but he'd heard her tell people it could be too quiet. They had lived there together all his life, and Matt knew she'd loved having him and Mahalia stay with her the past few weeks. He found it lonely too, bringing up a baby by himself. The flat had been unbearable after Emmy went, and that was one of the reasons he'd gone back to stay with his mother.

But he needed to strike out on his own again.

On the veranda floor he found a set of bamboo wind chimes lying abandoned like a collection of old bones. He picked it up and fixed some of the strings and hung it, and that night it sang them to sleep with its diffident music.

Matt liked his new place. He liked looking out through the gaps in the latticework that screened the veranda on one side, seeing the world chopped up into tiny squares. He liked the way the paint peeled off the door, showing layer upon layer going right back in time to a grim ocher. He liked looking out in the mornings to see the gray-bearded man from the 20,000 Cows Vegetarian Restaurant across the road eating breakfast, visible through the glass window of his shop. He liked the buzz of commercial activity: the service station across the road, the saddlery next door (WE TRAVEL TO FIT YOUR SADDLE said the sign), the paper shop on the next corner, and the pub down the street. He

43

even liked the rambling voices of drunks making their way home on foot after closing time, their bursts of song and equally brief bursts of argument. Most of all he liked the way you could see the country in the distance if you looked down the end of the street.

Daily life with a baby took up all his energy. Eliza spent a lot of her time at the Conservatorium, which was in an old high school building in the main street. She was a singing student, and worked at a café as a waitress, so he didn't see much of her at first. Dave moved out and Matt agreed with Eliza that they should try and let his room. So far there had been no takers.

He took Mahalia for walks. They went shopping and he bought things for them to eat. People walking past them often smiled at Mahalia. Sometimes they stopped to talk to him. Having a baby was the way to meet everyone in the world, eventually.

In this part of town, people were poor. You could see it in their dull lank hair and cheap clothing: chain-store flannelette shirts and track pants and sneakers. There were also hip young poor people in army-surplus greatcoats and boots and dreadlocks. But it all amounted to the same thing. Everyone, like Matt, was just getting by.

Mahalia enjoyed her walks in the windy spring sunshine. She kicked her legs and sucked on her fists. She laughed and talked to the universe. Matt answered her, saying, "Yes, that's a cat, a cat, Mahalia. Meow meow. And here are the dogs! Do you remember the dogs? Teg and Tessa. That's what they're called."

He stopped outside the Laundromat so Mahalia could reach out and touch the orange fur of the two chows that sat there hanging out their blue tongues and panting with happiness. He'd learned their names when he met their owner, who lived down the laneway beside the shops.

Mahalia squealed and lunged at the dogs. She sat back triumphantly with fur between her fingers and tried to put it in her mouth, but Matt patiently removed it and showed her how to pat the chows nicely. "Dad dad dad," she said, chomping her new teeth and her top gums together, lifting her chin and stretching out her hand.

They walked down to the paddock under the railway overpass, to visit the horses, and Matt lifted Mahalia out of the stroller and held her so she could pat them. Mahalia panted quickly with pleasure, a few loud huffs that made Matt sure she must be able to smell their strong, exciting, horsey smell.

Emmy had shown him a story she'd written when she was ten. She'd been ambitious then, and hadn't even thought of spending her school days sprawled on the riverbank, watching clouds.

She'd kept it all that time. Six years. It was a long story, with chapters.

It was about how she'd run away with her horse, called Flame. (The horse was made up. She didn't have a horse, had never had a horse, though she'd learned to ride at a friend's place.)

In the story she loaded Flame with a saddlebag full of food and a sleeping bag, and ran away to have an adventure, sleeping at night under the stars in front of her campfire. One day she saw headlines in the paper about a missing girl and horse who were wanted by the police, and rather than give herself up, she packed up at once and set off quickly so they couldn't find her, heading for Western Australia.

Mahalia

That was as much as she'd written. She'd illustrated it, with meticulously drawn pictures of horses, including saddles and bridles. Matt admired the determination of the girl in the story: not to be caught, to have adventures. He even admired her callousness in not worrying about her anxious parents.

"One day, Mahalia," he said, "you can have a horse. When Emmy comes back, we can live in the country with horses."

Oh motherless child-ren
 motherless chil-il-dren
 mother-less child-re-en
 have such a hard hard hard hard hard ti-i-i-ime
 And it's sometimes I feel
 I feel someti-ci-mes
 Like a motherless
 motherless chi-ild
 Oh and sometimes I feel I feel I feel
 like a mother-less
 motherless
 child
 A lo-ong way
 Such a long long way
 A lo-ong way
 Fro-om my ho-o-ome.

Matt stood in the dark center of the house and stared up the stairs to where Eliza was singing in the hallway of the second floor. The light coming down from the top of the house, the shadows everywhere, the stillness, and the purity of the sound made the broken-down old building feel like a cathedral.

It was a simple, dignified song, sung with strength and purpose. Eliza improvised and sang on, oblivious of Matt standing in the shadows, listening. She played with the notes, bent them and warbled them, whispered them and cried them out, her whole body, her mouth and lungs and chest an instrument for the sound.

When she'd finished, she continued on her way down the stairs, which was where she'd been going until a fit of singing overtook her. Eliza was heavy on her feet; she was one of those people whose footfalls sound heavily and resoundingly through a house. She arrived at the foot of the stairs with a jump and saw Matt, still standing where he'd been arrested by the sound.

"Hi," she said. Her hair was wet from a shower, and still dripping water. She smiled at him and went on into the kitchen.

Mahalia had been asleep in their room upstairs, and now she woke and started to cry, wanting Matt to come to her. He went up the stairs two at a time and caught her in his arms. When he arrived in the kitchen with Mahalia to make her a bottle, Eliza was sitting with her head flung forward, toweling her hair dry. Her knees were apart, her hair swept over her face from the back, and her neck was bare. She didn't see him come in, but she heard him and said, muffled by the towel, "I hope I didn't wake Mahalia up."

"She was due to wake anyway—doesn't sleep long during the day." Matt had only been in the house less than a week, and they were still at the stage of getting to know each other, polite, asking tentative questions, sounding each other out.

Eliza sat up and tossed her hair back from her face in a swift, practiced movement.

"Do you want the singing lesson?"

Matt measured milk powder into Mahalia's bottle. "You mean the optional free singing lesson that comes with the room?"

Eliza laughed. "Yeah, well, I thought it might be an added inducement. It's not the most attractive place to live, but I like it."

"I don't sing." He settled Mahalia onto his lap, where she lay back, sucking on her bottle.

"Oh, go on. You play the guitar, right? So you must sing along with it sometimes."

"I sound like someone being strangled."

But instead of protesting that he must be exaggerating, as many people would have, she said, "You're probably not using the right techniques."

Matt shook his head. "I'd never keep it up. But I could play my guitar while you sang. It's a bass, though."

"Yeah, I know, I've heard you playing in your room. Interesting to sing along with. I'll improvise."

Matt handed Mahalia to Eliza while he fetched his instrument. Mahalia wasn't yet shy of strangers, and Eliza smiled at her so winningly that Mahalia smiled and smiled back, with her milky, gummy mouth, and wouldn't drink any more of her bottle. So Eliza sat her up on her knee and got her a crust of bread to chew. When Matt came back with the guitar, they were both sitting there eating bread and butter.

"She needs to chew," said Eliza. "Now that she's got some teeth. Give her gums something to work on too. Do you have an amp?"

Matt shook his head. "My friend Otis does, and I plug it in when I go to his place."

"That's okay. You won't drown me out then."

Matt didn't think it would be possible to drown Eliza out. He'd heard how she could belt out a song. "How come you know so much about babies?" he said.

"My sister. I've been an aunt since I was twelve." She glanced at Matt's guitar case, on which Otis had lettered BLUES IS THE MUSIC THAT HEALS. "Who said that?"

"John Lee Hooker, I think."

"Mahalia Jackson wouldn't have agreed. She said that blues are the songs of despair. Gospel songs are the songs of hope. When you sing gospel, you have a feeling there's a cure for what's wrong."

Matt wasn't used to people talking this way: putting forward ideas, unafraid of what people would think. "How old are you, anyway?" he said.

"Twenty-two."

She handed Mahalia to Matt, who sat her on the floor and gave her some plastic containers to play with. Then he tuned his guitar for a bit, and when he was ready he picked out a soft, low rhythm that Eliza improvised to, making her voice deep and growly. They went on until Eliza started laughing so hard she had to stop.

"So you're at the Con," said Matt, after he'd relished the silence that filled the kitchen when they'd finished the song. "What's it like?" He put away his guitar and picked up Mahalia, sitting her on his knee.

"Oh, it's fantastic!" said Eliza. "Wonderful! It's what I've always wanted to do. But I never thought I'd have the chance to be a full-time singing student. When I left school, I did what I was only mildly interested in."

"What was that?"

"I became a hairdresser." Eliza grimaced, and laughed. "Yes, look at me now—I just let my hair grow out long and frizzy the way nature intended it. Cut it myself when it gets too unruly.

"But to spend most of my day singing . . . it's a dream come true. Have to pinch myself sometimes. All those years I spent making tea for customers and sweeping hair from the floor and snipping away . . ." She did an exaggerated shudder. "I never want to do it again. I waitress now, to get money, rather than do that again." Her voice was puzzled. "I always kind of liked fiddling with people's hair when I was a kid. But not as much as singing. Funny, isn't it?"

Eliza reached for an orange from a bowl, peeled it with her hands, and ate it a segment at a time, not worrying about the juice that covered her fingers. "D'you mind me asking," she said, "how come you're looking after Mahalia on your own? I mean, it's a bit unusual."

Matt took a breath. This was the question people would always ask. "Oh, Emmy found it really hard with a baby and she needed a break." He grasped Mahalia's foot and counted her toes off, one at a time, wiggling them as he went. She laughed and kicked her legs, because it tickled.

He hadn't even explained to himself *how come* yet.

Eliza noticed his awkwardness and left it alone. She said, "That song I was singing on my way down the stairs . . . I didn't think . . . I didn't mean to be tactless. . . . *Motherless child* could be interpreted as someone without a mother country. It could be about the Negroes longing for Africa. Or for heaven."

She held out her arms to take Mahalia, and it seemed the most natural thing in the world for Matt to hand her over for a while. She said, "Sometimes I think we're all a long way from home."

Mahalia

* * *

Matt wrote to Emmy at last. *Mahalia is well*, he said, *and we are both missing you. We are living in town, but when you come back we could get a place in the bush and have horses.*

Then he crumpled the letter up, switched off the light, and lay watching the shadows on the ceiling. Mahalia was sleeping in her crib; he heard her snuffle and sigh. He strained to listen to her breath. Sometimes he suffered from such anxiety for her that he feared that she would simply stop breathing one night; he'd heard that some babies do. If she coughed in her sleep, he woke and listened, afraid that she might be getting sick.

There were flickering shadows from the streetlights, and a car roared past. Gusts of wind rattled the chimes on the veranda. Mahalia woke and started to cry, a sad, sorry-for-herself cry; Matt picked her up at once and buried his face in the sweet-smelling down on top of her head. He changed her diaper and took her downstairs to warm a bottle, and she settled down at last in the darkness to serious, intent drinking.

Afterward, still unable to sleep, Matt bundled them both up and settled Mahalia into her stroller and set off for a long walk. These walks were becoming a habit for him.

They passed other night walkers and exchanged curt greetings.

"G'd'evening."

"G'd'evening."

Matt's voice was always gruffer than he felt. He passed through the main street, where kids in hotted-up cars loitered after the pubs had shut, and girls with short skirts leaned against cars, just hanging out, not wanting to go home.

A black dog followed them, joining them from a shadowy gateway not far from where they lived. It was like a spirit-dog at first, keeping a distance from them, so that Matt could imagine that it was a hallucination, an imaginary dog. And then it came closer, huffing a warm doggy breath near the backs of his knees and glancing up at him with that craven devotion that dogs assume. *Voucher*, Matt called it, and the dog pricked up its ears as if this were a name it could recognize.

Matt walked for hours along suburban streets and along the riverbank that he and Emmy had once made their own. Life went on, all through the night. He saw aimless kids in track pants and baseball hats wandering with nothing to do, drawn together by some kind of fellow feeling, diverging in a wandering orbit for a while and then accidentally-on-purpose bumping into each other, rattling against each other, looking for something, or for trouble, whichever came first. He saw police cars cruise by, and, once, a woman cowering in the bushes outside her house with her children while a drunken husband ranted and raved inside. He saw lovers, lingering hand in hand or parked in cars, not wanting to part, or with nowhere else to go. He was part of that aimless, nighttime other-life, because he didn't want to lie sleepless listening to Mahalia's breath and thinking of Emmy. He walked rhythmically, listening to the whisper of the stroller's wheels on the pavement, the sighs from Mahalia as she slept, the click of the dog's claws following on the concrete. The silence was broken by the slam of a car door, a raised voice, or a car roaring past. Sometimes Mahalia woke, and Matt became aware of her eyes staring darkly out into the night before the lids drooped again and closed. Plump-jowled, her head lolled to the side. Matt walked, and every footstep, every creak and movement of his shoes said *Emmy, Emmy, Emmy.*

In the white room with bare walls and tall windows of frosted glass, Emmy had slept and slept.

Nothing seemed to ease her tiredness, not even when they changed Mahalia over to bottle feeding and Matt got up with her at night. In the morning he woke to Mahalia's voice and took her into bed with them, where she and Matt lay beside the sleeping Emmy and looked at the white light coming through glass as beaded as a cold bottle.

It was a white, dazzling room with splintered sunlight.

"What will you do?" said Emmy, sitting at the table, her feet still in bedsocks.

Matt shook his head. He had no idea. She meant *for a job,* and he felt defeated already. He'd left school too soon and there seemed nothing he wanted to do anyway.

Through the wall they could hear the old woman whose half-house they rented moving about making tea. Her kettle screamed and was choked off. Matt got to his feet and grabbed his guitar.

"Got to go and see Otis," he said, kissing Emmy on her cool forehead and slipping guiltily down the wooden stairs at the back of the flat.

When he got home later, it was twilight on a chilly overcast afternoon and the flat was dark and silent. Emmy was in bed; she woke when he came in, and was as dazed as a sleepwalker. Mahalia's crib was empty.

There was a sound like a mouse at the back door, a kind of

humble furtive scratching. It was Jean, the old woman they rented from, with a sleeping Mahalia bundled in her arms. "I thought I heard you come in, dear," she said. "Tell Emmy she was as good as gold all afternoon." Matt took his baby from her, ashamed of his absence, determined that no near-strangers would be asked to look after Mahalia ever again.

It wasn't long after that that Emmy said, "I think I need to go away for a while." It was more decisive than anything she'd said in a long time.

The wheels of Mahalia's stroller whirred along the lamp-lit pavement. It was down there, down that street they'd just passed, that they'd all lived together.

When they approached home, the dog peeled off into its own yard and disappeared like an apparition. Matt maneuvered the stroller in through the front door. There was a pale light in the sky; he'd walked longer than usual and it was almost morning. He settled Mahalia into her crib, and she sighed heavily and rolled over onto her side. Matt felt his bed was woefully empty of Emmy. He tried to imagine what she might be doing and feeling. Did she miss him, or Mahalia? Matt tried to imagine her. It was becoming harder and harder. He couldn't think of the whole Emmy, just bits and pieces that came into his memory, suddenly and painfully.

Emmy had a shoal of freckles on her body. She was speckled like a trout. Sometimes Matt had imagined that her skin would suddenly burst into color, a color that moved and shifted like a tide, waves of blue and pink.

7

Matt woke late, coming up into the light like a diver from the sea. The wind chimes rattled, a hollow reedy knock that came and went with the gusts of wind. But that wasn't what had woken him. There was a steady pounding at the front door. He scooped a drowsy Mahalia up from her crib and went down to open it.

"Hey, I'm Virginia." The person at the door turned from surveying the street, smiled, and held out her hand, looking shyly from under a baseball cap. Matt took the hand and shook it. He had been uncertain at first whether she was a man or a woman. She was dressed in androgynous clothing, cord pants, and a tracksuit top, and she was tall and thin and somewhat stooped.

"Virginia?" he said stupidly, still half-asleep.

"I've come about the room? Gee, did I wake you? It's such a big place and I wanted someone to hear. . . ." She gestured nervously with a thin hand. "Is the room still for rent?"

"Um, yeah, no one's taken the room yet, but Eliza, she's the one you should see. I think she's probably gone already. . . . But maybe you should come in anyway," he offered, and Virginia stepped inside.

"Hey, this your baby? She's beautiful." Virginia had teeth that protruded at the top, and an endearing way of bobbing her head and peering out from under her cap. Mahalia grasped a finger of Virginia's outstretched hand; she was better at waking up than Matt, and always ready for company.

Virginia spoke quickly, hardly pausing between sentences. "See, I'm living over at the trailer park. I came up from Sydney—I'm supposed to be doing this TAFE course, but it's so boring—it's not really what I want to do. Anyway, thought I'd be better off in a house, and the room here's cheaper than the trailer?" The ends of her sentences often went up into a question.

"Hey, I'm talking all the time, you got to stop me," she said with a dismissive wave of her hands. They were in the kitchen now, and Matt had put the kettle on. "Yeah, I'd love a cup of tea."

Virginia stopped talking and took a long look at Matt. She lifted up the baseball cap and pushed her hair behind her ears. The action accentuated her long face, the face of a faithful hound, stolid and rather dreamy.

"I just don't want to live with junkies again," she said. "Got a room a while back and we all got chucked out by the agent a few weeks later. I was givin' the other people my rent every week and they were shooting it up. You're not mixed up with that stuff? Sorry, but I just want to be careful."

Matt shook his head.

Virginia shifted her weight from foot to foot and looked away from Matt's face. "Anyway, maybe I should come back when this Eliza's home."

"Don't you want to see the room?"

"Yeah. Oh, yeah, okay." Matt led her up the stairs. "I really like it around here, you know? That pub on the corner has really cheap meals. I eat there when I can—couldn't cook it myself for what they sell it for there. . . ."

Dave's old room was small and looked over the square of backyard and Eliza's vegetable garden. A pumpkin vine grew over the back fence, and it had a butternut pumpkin on it. Virginia peered out through the back window as she talked. "See, I really wanted to do this media course at the uni, but they didn't let me in. Said I hadn't done enough school, but all I want to do is make films, you know?" She shook her head at the impossibility of it all. "So now I'm doing this TAFE course, trying to get my Year 12 certificate. Maybe I'd be better off just getting myself a camera, making films on my own."

"Thanks," she said when they were back in the kitchen again. She looked bashful. "Look, I talk too much, you gotta stop me. Maybe you can tell that girl that I came by. Eliza, was it? Yeah. Maybe I'll come back later? Anyway, look, I've gotta go, gotta go, I'll see you round the place, eh?"

She took off, clumping out through the front room. Matt heard the door close behind her.

Mahalia started to fuss for her bottle, so Matt sat her on the worn linoleum so that he could prepare it. "Gotta get you a high chair, mate," he said. "You can't spend your life groveling round everyone's feet."

Matt hocked his guitar. The money he got from the pension was never enough. Sometimes it simply disappeared on him and he didn't know where it had gone. He tried making lists of what he spent it on. Food, powdered baby formula, rent, power, disposable diapers when he was feeling lazy, chocolate bars to keep his energy up. He saw how easy it was for money to go. It all added up.

He thought he could do without the guitar for a while. He would save to get it out of hock. Or he'd come up with a job, soon. A part-time job, at least. Anyway, if he lost it, he'd get another guitar. One day.

But it seemed like a bit of himself disappearing when he handed the black case over the counter, BLUES IS THE MUSIC THAT HEALS lettered in Otis's writing on the side, the white paint so thick it was textured like an oil painting.

Matt discovered that *waiting room* was an accurate description of the outer public area of a doctor's office. He waited and waited there one day with Mahalia, after her bogus, attention-getting cough turned into a real one. Her nose continually ran with thick yellow snot, and she didn't sleep for more than an hour at a time. Matt hadn't slept for three nights by the time he waited in the waiting room, patting Mahalia on the back and talking to her in an attempt to stop her pathetic cry.

It was a gray, miserable room on a gray, miserable day, a rainy spring day that felt like winter. The chairs had hairy gray seats and every one of them was occupied. Matt preferred to stand and move about with Mahalia curled against his shoulder. He listened to the coughs and noticed the hairy patterns on people's sweaters, the hairiness of their winter coats. His world had turned into a gray, hairy, coughing, sniffling, waiting one.

All the doctor could do was reassure him that Mahalia didn't have an infection, and all that could be done was to make her more comfortable. He wrote down the names of things Matt could get at the drugstore to ease her congestion. He was a kind man, with a waiting room full of coughing patients he couldn't do much for.

Matt took Mahalia to visit Otis. He really wanted Charmian to fuss over Mahalia for a while, and look after her for him, and she did.

"How's my baby girl?" said Charmian. "Not feelin' too well, eh?" She rubbed Mahalia's chest with baby eucalyptus rub that she kept for her grandchildren. Mahalia's grizzles subsided; she arched her back and stuck her tummy out, squirming with pleasure as Charmian's plump hands continued to massage her chest.

"Your auntie Charmian'll make you better."

Otis tossed a cap onto his head and grinned at Matt. He squinted into the mirror in the hallway and changed the angle of it, flashing his eyes at his own reflection. Otis had thinned down lately; he went running with his father and rode his bike around just for the exercise. There were hollows in his cheeks that hadn't been there before.

"You're starting to look sharp," said Matt. "You after someone or something?"

"Let's go for a walk," said Otis, giving Matt a smile that told him he wasn't going to let on. "Won't be long, Auntie!" he called, and they let themselves out the front door.

"My life is shit at the moment," said Matt. "Ever since Emmy left . . ." He shoved his hands into his pockets, wishing his jeans weren't stiff with grime. *I have to go to the Laundromat, have to get things together, have to stop wasting my time, get a job, write to Emmy; got to make it all WORK!*

The night dog, Voucher, came along the street and ran up to

Matt, tail wagging. "Hey," laughed Otis. "This dog knows you! Where you live, eh, where you live?" he asked the dog. Otis had a way with dogs; he swore they talked to him.

Eliza's ad for the room had said FRIENDLY HOUSEHOLD. And Eliza was friendly. She picked Mahalia up and crooned to her, and told Matt to help himself from the VEGGIE GARDEN that she'd also mentioned in the ad.

The veggie garden was a raised bed in the middle of a concrete space at the back of the building, and contained mostly herbs, plus a few frilly lettuces and a single tomato plant.

After a long day at the Con, Eliza dumped her bag on the kitchen table and waltzed on her bare feet out to her plot, where she squatted and weeded and watered until dark. She had a compost heap in the corner that she cared for as tenderly as the garden itself.

But, friendly as she was, Eliza wasn't often at home. Matt felt at times that he and Mahalia inhabited the entire dark building on their own. The shadows sometimes spooked him. It was tedious looking after a baby, and he thought of Emmy often. He thought of her mouth as it was when he had first met her: generous and smiling. He refused images of her as she had become after Mahalia was born, when her forehead creased into a frown and she didn't smile much at all. But memories were relentless, and sometimes he just had to get out of the house, so he walked, not really caring where. The movement made him feel better.

One day, late in the afternoon, he found himself at the place where Eliza was a student. It was a former high school in the center of town, two tall ramshackle brick buildings in an asphalt parking lot. Fig trees and camphor-laurels provided shelter, so

Mahalia

Matt sat on a seat underneath them. Graffiti on a wall of the building asked the passerby to SUBVERT THE DOMINANT PARADIGM. It also said EJACAYSHUN FOR ALL, NOT JUST THE RICHÉ, and WHY SO MANY POOR? Mahalia chewed on her fist and grizzled; she was getting her top front teeth.

Young people dressed in glitzy rag-bag clothes, clothes like Eliza's, greeted each other and bounded up and down the stairs. With their colored hair and jewelry they made Matt feel dun-colored. They were as casual as birds, but they had purpose.

Crows gathered in the fig trees and squabbled, dropping fruits to the ground. Their voices were harsh and lonely. Matt looked up to the top of the building and saw fig seedlings growing in the gutters. It felt as if the end of the world had come and Nature was reasserting herself. The students were the bright, feral remnants of a society that had destroyed itself.

From inside the building he heard the beat of a drum, and then someone starting to sing. It sounded like Eliza's voice. Tired of sitting and listening to Mahalia fuss, Matt carried her stroller up the steps at the back of the building.

Inside, the walls were painted in bright colors, hung with artwork. A gray metal tray for smokers overflowed with plastic drink bottles and lollipop wrappers. Matt couldn't hear the singing now that he was inside, but he wandered up stairs and down corridors, wheeling the stroller over a coarse old blue carpet that flowed like a river through the building, up and down staircases that linked various mezzanine floors. It was a labyrinth, with colored glass windows throwing eerie light over the floor. The bones of the old school building it had once been were there, but it looked like a place that had been settled by gypsies.

Matt saw a young man with a shaved head striding along a corridor. "Hello!" the man called. "Hello!"

"Hello!" A voice came from inside a room somewhere. Eliza's voice. Matt recognized it, and something inside him leapt with happiness that at last there was something familiar to him in this strange place.

"Hello!"

"Hello!"

The voices continued trying to locate each other, while Matt followed along the corridor.

And Eliza emerged from a classroom, almost bumping into the man with the shaved head, a wide smile on her face. She hugged him quickly.

And then she saw Matt, and Mahalia, and she hugged Matt, too. She squatted down to say hello to Mahalia, who stopped her fussing and lunged with delight at Eliza, straining against the stroller's seat belt, patting Eliza on the face with her damp little hands.

But despite Mahalia's charms, Eliza went off with the man with the shaved head, whose name was Brent, or Trent, or Kent, who had bright dark eyes like raisins, and an echoing black mole on the side of his face. Matt was surprised to find himself left with a strong feeling of disappointment. He watched as they walked away, saw Eliza shove her friend playfully and laugh at something that he'd said.

Matt looked down at Mahalia, who sat playing with her toes. He felt desolate. There wasn't much *fun* in his life. He couldn't simply stroll off with someone and do whatever he felt like.

Matt pushed the stroller back home, over the bridge with the metal walkway, past the trendy pub where gay people hung out, and down their street of peeling timber houses, the front yards littered with discarded chip packets. He bought a loaf of bread on the way and ate it while he walked. Matt was often ravenous, and bread filled him. Mahalia chewed on the crusts, biting down with her almost-through teeth.

Matt threw himself onto the bed. He longed for his guitar— he could always do *that* and satisfy some itch in himself—but it was gone, locked away in the hock shop, waiting for him to find the money to get it out again.

Mahalia rolled about on the floor. She was good at rolling— front to back, and back to front again. She could sit well now, as long as Matt sat her up first.

"You'll be crawling soon, Mahalia."

She turned to his voice and smiled.

A letter arrived from Emmy, addressed to his mother's place. She brought it round one day but he didn't want to open it in front of her, so he dropped it onto the table. To Matt, it seemed to burn there.

"Is there anything you need? Any way I can help?" His mother had taken Mahalia onto her hip, and jiggled her up and down as she spoke. Her offers were always too casual. He felt like a horse she didn't want to frighten. He knew this was because he'd been so insistent that he care for Mahalia by himself, wanting to show everyone, himself included, that he could do it.

"No thanks," said Matt. "We're all right."

"Aw, Matt," said his mother in an exaggerated pleading voice, trying to make a joke of it, "*Let* me have her for a couple of days—I'd love to look after her, give you a break. Everyone with a baby needs a break!" She addressed the last remark looking into Mahalia's eyes, who smiled at her and giggled.

Matt smiled and pretended he hadn't heard her. He could be stubborn, and proud. Alone at last with Mahalia, he opened the letter.

Emmy hoped they were well. She thought of Mahalia. Knew Matt would be looking after her. She couldn't come back just yet. She was sorry.

Emmy always put a circle for a period and over the letter *i*. She used a little *i* instead of a capital when she meant herself.

Virginia came back at a time when Eliza was there and Matt agreed for her to join them. Eliza was democratic. There weren't a lot of takers anyway for the empty room, despite the FRIENDLY HOUSEHOLD and the VEGGIE GARDEN and the OPTIONAL FREE SINGING LESSONS.

Virginia was warm and easygoing and idealistic, but talkative. She raved on about everything. (*Man!* said Otis after he'd met her. *She sure goes on!*) She went on about politics, about the drug problem, about how all she wanted to do was to make documentary films about the way kids lived on the streets, shaking her head in bemusement at the shortcomings of society. She laughed and smiled just as readily, though, and Matt didn't mind having her around at all.

Mahalia had entered a shy stage, aware that she was a distinct person from everyone else around her. She was wary of this new person at first, turning her head away if Virginia spoke directly to her. But soon she allowed Virginia to feed her, laughing so hard at the faces she pulled that mashed vegetables spilled from her mouth and splattered onto the tray of her high chair.

The house didn't spook Matt so much now that Virginia was there. He doubted that she ever did go to the TAFE course she was supposed to be doing. She hung about the house all day. "Mind if I come in?" she'd say, standing tentatively at the doorway of Matt's room, then coming in with two cups of coffee and lowering herself onto the floor. Mahalia could push herself about on her stomach now, and she moved over to where Virginia sat and thumped her with a fat hand. "Ow," said Virginia, pulling a face, and Mahalia laughed and hit her again.

"Brute! You're a little brute!" said Virginia, rolling her over onto her back and lifting up Mahalia's singlet to kiss her on the belly button.

Matt looked away. Emmy used to rub her pregnant belly with olive oil. It was a graceful, heavy shape, like a droplet of water, but with a tracery of blue veins. Her belly button had popped out, an untidy knot of skin.

"You know, I'd like to have a baby," Virginia told Matt. "Someone of my own to look after. I reckon it'd be all right, you know?" She shrugged. "But . . . it'll never happen."

"You never know," said Matt.

Virginia shook her head. "Nah," she said. "How old you reckon I am?"

Matt shook his head. *Twenty-five*, he thought, but didn't say. Sometimes he thought Virginia seemed seventeen, same age as him, she was so shy and goofy and young-looking. But she had tiny wrinkles round her eyes.

"I'm thirty-four," she said. "And I've never met anyone yet I'd want to have a baby with. It'll never happen."

Mahalia

Matt recognized the phrase. *It'll never happen.* Sometimes he thought that about himself, about lots of things. About getting a job. About playing bass in a band. About Emmy coming back.

It'll never happen.

But Mahalia had happened. He was still sometimes astonished at her existence.

Life in the house was often a series of random meetings that took place in the bathroom or kitchen. "Just a minute, Matt, I'll be out of the shower in a minute!" Eliza and Virginia were very different. Eliza was all curly hair and womanly curves and lacy frocks she'd found at thrift shops and Virginia was narrow-hipped and boyish and sauntering. Eliza tore through the house on her way to or from various obligations and assignations, and Virginia at first peered warily at her from under the visor of her cap, trying to figure her out, but soon came to like her.

"There's half a cheesecake from my coffee shop in the fridge. It's still perfectly all right, just a bit old to sell, but I told them my gorgeous flatmates would scoff it!" Eliza would call out as she let herself out the front door, on her way to somewhere in a hurry. Or: "I found this at the thrift shop, thought it looked like you," handing Virginia a fleecy top. "No, don't bother," waving away Virginia's offer of money. "It was only a buck." Virginia, because she was more often at home, thought to do things like bring Eliza's washing in when it rained, and Eliza appreciated it. One night, when Eliza sat, exhausted, with her head on the kitchen table, Virginia quietly brought her a cup of tea.

"You know, mate," she told Eliza gently, "you should seriously think about not burning the candle at both ends."

They were good at annoying each other too. "D'you think that Virginia could find any *more* stray people than she does?" Eliza asked Matt grumpily one morning, after a shy girl with long dark hair had made her way out of the bathroom. When Eliza was annoyed, it was always *that Virginia*.

"I reckon I'll just chuck the lot out!" said Virginia with disgust one day, looking at the festering, half-empty cartons of Eliza's yogurt that cluttered the fridge.

Matt simply watched the two of them, bemused. He caught snatches of conversations that he could never be part of: ". . . because I've got an itchy *fanny!*" Eliza called to Virginia, disappearing into the backyard to tend her herb garden.

They all put in money for "basics," but apart from that they mostly looked after themselves. Because he had Mahalia, Matt was the only one who cooked properly all the time. Virginia appeared to live on baked beans, sometimes straight from the can ("Ya don't notice what ya eating when ya hungry"), or went to the pub on the corner for a cheap meal when she had the money. Eliza often ate on the run whatever she found in the fridge, cramming food into her mouth with her fingers, standing at the kitchen sink.

When Eliza was at home, she was never still. She strode quickly with heavy footsteps down hallways and stairs, making the treads shudder. She whooshed the taps on in the bathroom as she washed out her underwear in the sink, singing all the while, and accidentally squirting water everywhere. She ran out with handfuls of dripping cloth to the backyard, where she hung her knickers on the line that stretched across the small space. She chopped vegetables with great vigor on the kitchen table, often neglecting to use the chopping board, so that the laminated surface was feathered with tiny cuts. She whizzed up fruit smoothies in the blender and slurped them down, wiping her mouth with the back of her hand. Matt became used to the sight of her long back whisking round corners, her lace dress flapping round her ankles and feet.

On one of the rare occasions that he found her still, sitting at the kitchen table with a cup of herbal tea, she said, "Hey, get your guitar, let's have a jam; you play, I'll sing."

Matt said, "I can't. I've pawned it."

Eliza looked at him for a moment, then finished her tea in a long gulp and scooped the herbal tea bag out of the bottom of the cup with her fingers.

"That's a shame," she said. But she was used to people resorting to desperate measures. She'd have pawned her own voice sometimes if she'd been able to.

"Pawned it?" said Otis. "Shit, man." He handed Matt an old acoustic belonging to his father. "This is a crap guitar, but it's something to play on." It wasn't a bass, but it would have to do. Matt tuned it.

Charmian stood smoking, holding her cigarette out the window between puffs, pretending she wasn't smoking inside.

"Hey, Matt," she said, "you ever read the Bible?" Charmian had a sincere and unswerving belief in the capacity of the Bible to help people.

"No," said Matt.

"It's the Truth, that book," she said seriously. "You betta read it, boy. You should bring that baby girl of yours up a Christian."

Matt smiled and strummed a few chords.

Charmian's grandchildren were visiting. They roughed around with Mahalia on the floor. Mahalia loved it: she came up panting for air and then hurled herself forward on top of them again.

Alan came in and Charmian threw the cigarette out the window. He sniffed suspiciously. "Who's been smoking in here?"

"Now I'm going to pick up my baby," said Charmian airily, ignoring him and plucking Mahalia out of the scrum of children. Mahalia didn't like strangers now, but Charmian was no stranger, and she smiled at her and reached out to tug at her hair.

Matt hitched up to his mother's place, because he wanted to escape from town for a bit, and because he knew she liked him to visit. He got lonely for someone he was connected to. Otis and Alan and Charmian were good to visit but they still weren't his family.

It was that day, watching her grandmother drink a cup of tea, that Mahalia decided she would like to drink from a cup. She reached toward it, grunting and stretching out her hands. Matt's mother got up and fetched an old plastic cup of Matt's that had been in the cupboard all this time, and gave her some water in it.

Mahalia put her mouth to the lip of the cup eagerly, and Matt tipped it up. Water ran down her chin, but she managed to swallow some. She looked up at Matt and smiled, thumping her hand on the table, she was so delighted with herself. Later, when Matt offered her milk in a bottle, she waved it away, so he offered her the cup with some milk in it, and she drank, licking her lips and lifting her eyes up to him, showing that she wanted more.

Now that she could drag herself across the floor, it was impossible to keep her clean, for the floors at Matt's place were ingrained with dirt. The pink singlet that she wore was covered with black grime, and so were her hands and face. She was happy and filthy.

While Matt was outside wandering in the garden, his mother bathed her and dressed her in a new playsuit she'd bought. As she was doing up the buttons, she saw Matt leaning against the doorway, watching. She sat Mahalia in the middle of the floor with some plastic blocks and took her dirty things out to the laundry, where she soaked them in a bucket.

"I think you should take Mahalia to see Emmy's parents," she said briskly and conversationally when she returned. "I'm sure they'd like to see her."

Matt thought about what she'd said. "Well, you're probably right," he said after a while. "After Emmy had her they only saw her once or twice. Emmy never wanted to go to them."

"There could be lots of reasons for that—Emmy was always fighting them, wasn't she? And, okay, I know they were hard on her too. But you know, it's not just for them, but for Mahalia. Children need grandparents.

"You could have done with some," she added, looking half-ashamed. "But I didn't have any say in the matter. My parents were dead."

Matt formed a sentence in his mind that he thought he could speak if he got up the courage. Something had been worrying him for some time. "They couldn't—you know—take her away?"

It was something he dreaded. Such things, he'd felt up to now, were better not voiced. But he'd known all along that there were other people who might make a claim on Mahalia, and he needed to know the possibilities.

"Of course not," she said. "Emmy left her with you. And you're her father, you have the most claim on her—you and Emmy. You're not neglecting her, so they'd have no grounds to take her. Anyhow, I don't think they'd want to. Raise a baby. At their age?"

After a while he said, "And what about Emmy? If she decided she didn't want to be with me but she wanted Mahalia back?"

His mother hesitated, looked down at the surface of the table and then back at his face. "That would be more difficult," she said. "She's Mahalia's mother."

Eliza bought herself an old bicycle. Matt would see her riding round town in shorts and Blundstone boots, with shopping bags full of vegetables over the handlebars. She rode effortlessly and quickly, bike wheels whizzing over the roads, unaware of anyone looking at her. People were drawn to her look of careless confidence, and then they looked at her long legs and clever, dreamy lion's face.

Matt got used to the bicycle in the front room. He looked forward to seeing it there. He would come through the front door, dragging Mahalia's stroller over the threshold, and think, *Ah! Eliza's home!*

In the kitchen Eliza sat at the table and shelled peas. She sat with her legs apart, using her skirt as a receptacle for the shells. Her neck, bare because her hair was caught up in a knot on top of her head, bent forward over the task.

Matt washed dishes.

"It's probably none of my business, but," said Eliza, "I can't help wondering. . . . Did you intend to have a baby so early in your life?"

"Not really," Matt replied. "It just sort of happened."

He thought, then, that a lot of his life had just *sort of happened* to him. But now that Mahalia was here, he wanted her—the part of his life that concerned her, at least—to be deliberate.

"Anyway," he said, "don't most people just let things happen to them? Do you think your parents meant to have you?"

"I don't know," said Eliza. "I was the last one. Maybe . . ." She shrugged. "I haven't asked them. They never seem to speak to each other, and I don't have a lot to say to them either. I think I was a final thought. Or as people say, 'a mistake.'"

Matt turned back to the sink. He didn't like to think of Mahalia as *a mistake*. It was true that she was unintended, but they'd decided to keep her, hadn't they? They'd said that they'd *just love her, okay?*

As he worked, Matt listened for Mahalia, in case she woke. He finished washing the dishes and sat down at the table. Eliza handed him a pod that she'd split open, and he took it and licked the peas out with his tongue. She watched him and handed him another, just like that, casually, as though they'd known each other for years and didn't need to talk. The peas were sweet and cool on his tongue, and some were so tiny and unformed that they popped in his mouth. It was like eating pale green fish eggs, flavored like grass.

Once, Emmy jumped into the Richmond River fully clothed. She was there, beside him, on the grassy bank, and then suddenly she was in the water. The water she'd jumped into closed over her.

And then she was coming up for air, her mouth gasping like a fish, her hair streaming out behind her.

The Richmond River was a treacherous place, old and dirty. There were snags under the water, old tree branches with limbs supplicating like drowned men; dead dogs sometimes; old wharves covered in vines, their timbers rotten and spongy.

As she climbed out of the water, the freckles on her back showed through the wet thin cotton of her shirt. She laughed when Matt rubbed her arms, which were covered in goose bumps, even though she swore she wasn't cold.

She said she'd done it out of curiosity. To see what it felt like. She laughed.

Matt hadn't ever imagined that Emmy would jump into the river out of sheer curiosity. Once, he'd felt that he and Emmy were one person. But he was wrong.

Matt wanted to look after Mahalia without help from anyone, even though he knew his mother would love to take her for a day or two, and Charmian would be happy to have her there as part of the shifting throng of children she cared for from time to time. He didn't want to ask for any help at all. And he hadn't. He felt it would be a sign of failure to ask for help.

He loved Mahalia. Of course he loved her. But he got tired, and bored sometimes. Eliza might sing to her in a spare moment and Virginia sit and play or spoon food into her mouth, but in the end caring for Mahalia was always his responsibility.

One day, when everyone else was out and the house seemed full of ghosts again, Matt wandered about restlessly. He had put Emmy's letter away under his clothes; it haunted him, but he couldn't bear either to read it again or destroy it. He hadn't felt able to reply.

Late-afternoon sunlight made particles of dust dance down the stairs, and it was so still that even the wind chimes had taken a break. Mahalia was asleep. Her hands were flung in an attitude of abandon beside her face, which was as fat and shapeless in sleep as an old man's. Her eyelids flickered; perhaps she was dreaming.

Matt wandered out to the backyard and squatted down to look at Eliza's herbs. He reached out and pinched a leaf of a musky plant, putting it to his nostrils.

It was Friday night, the time when people went out to see their friends, ate food they hadn't had to cook, had a few drinks. Sometimes Matt experienced a great hunger, a need for a *good feed*, and he felt that need most urgently now. There was no decent food in the house. He craved bacon, and eggs, something greasy and salty and filling. There was nothing in the house that would satisfy that kind of hunger.

He got up quickly and went up to check on Mahalia. She hadn't had her after-lunch nap today, and had fallen asleep at last in the late afternoon. She was breathing quietly, her face abandoned to sleep. It wouldn't take him long to nip out to the corner shop and get some food to cook.

He hesitated. He'd never left her alone before, and he knew he shouldn't. Anything could happen while he was away. It wouldn't, but it could. But the shop was only a minute away. He pulled on a jacket and left the house quietly, pulling the door shut as stealthily and guiltily as a thief.

But once out, alone and unburdened for the first time since he could remember, his thoughts turned to the cheap burgers at the pub up the road. He could get a take-away and be away just a few minutes more than if he'd gone to the shop. It would be a fast mission—a mission for a hamburger. A bacon-and-egg burger. Saliva spurted shamefully into his mouth at the thought.

"Hey . . . mate!" It was Janno, one of the friends who'd melted away after Mahalia had been born. "Hey, come and sit down. We're all here. . . ."

Matt let himself be drawn away from the food counter to the beer garden at the back, thinking, *Just a moment. I'll say hello to everyone and just get back.* And he found his back slapped, and then he was sitting down, and everyone was laughing and someone put a beer in front of him and he took a sip.

And he drank the whole beer, thinking all the time *Just one more minute.* And then he was told how someone had a car and it was a *real beast* and someone else had a motorbike. *Filthy!*

And somehow it was good just to laugh and forget about things for a while, and he did, and then his beer was finished and someone was suggesting that he have another one. . . .

But he got to his feet and dragged himself away to their good-natured jeers and catcalls, but reluctantly, because he wanted to stay and drink and just *forget* for once. . . .

The streetlights were on, must have flickered on while he was inside, unaware of how dark it was getting. He ran up the dark road, food forgotten, thinking of the dark house, his thoughts dark and pounding through his head.

When he got there, the house wasn't dark; there was someone

there, and Mahalia was screaming, and her screams sounded all the way down the stairs. Virginia carried her, talking to her and patting her back, but she wouldn't stop crying.

Mahalia's face was damp and accusing, and she lunged from Virginia's arms to his. Her eyes were swollen and mottled, and her breath came in gasps.

"Hey, mate, what happened?" said Virginia. "I got home a minute ago and she was screaming her head off and the house was dark and she was alone. . . ."

She stopped herself from saying more.

"You know," she told Matt, "if you wanted to go out for a while, you should have asked when I got back. You just have to ask, you know."

Matt held Mahalia's cheek against his face. *I'm sorry, sorry, sorry*, said his heartbeat.

On a day in the middle of spring, an ordinary day when he woke to the predictable rattle of the wind chimes and Eliza singing in the bathroom, a day when Virginia's throaty laugh could be heard somewhere downstairs, when the front door slammed in the wind and someone shouted something unintelligible outside, Matt finally put Mahalia into her stroller in the middle of the afternoon and walked out into a world marked unexpectedly by wonder.

The last couple of weeks had been wet and gloomy after a rainy, influenza-filled winter, but today there was a breeze that blew the scent of orange blossom and jasmine through the air, and every single person Matt passed smiled at him and at Mahalia, and he had a feeling of undifferentiated sensuality and—yes!—sexiness that was directed at no one in particular but rather at the whole world.

Everyone was affected by the unexpected warmth, the scent of flowers that filled the streets, and by the luck of being alive at this particular moment in this particular place. People sat and chatted to their friends in outdoor cafés, and Matt saw plenty of people he knew, but he only stopped for a moment to say hello to them, for he was heading off to find Eliza at the Con.

There were two girls with baskets full of cellophane-wrapped rosebuds, giving them out free in the street, as a promotion for a florist. "Gee, thanks!" people said, and walked on. Young people, kids like Matt with no money, said to each other, "Hey, are they giving them out for nothing?" and ran to get one.

"Get me one too!" yelled their friends.

One of the girls stopped to offer one to Matt, smiling at Mahalia (*everyone* smiled at Mahalia!): he accepted it and walked on, feeling enchanted, walking on air.

Outside the redbrick building of the Con, Matt came across Charmian standing in the street, puffing on a cigarette, her legs as sturdy and solid as a tree deeply rooted in the ground. Her belly stuck out confidently with such a *don't care!* look and with such an air of belonging exactly to that spot that Matt waltzed up to her and handed her the rosebud, gallantly, though at the back of his mind he'd been saving it for Eliza.

She thanked him with great seriousness and tickled Mahalia under the arms. Mahalia squirmed back in her stroller, almost curling up into a ball with pleasure. Then Charmian gestured toward an old Falcon station wagon parked in the street with a FOR SALE sign on the back and asked Matt what he reckoned they'd want for it. "I have no idea," he said, and then he thought about it. "Couple of thousand?"

"But, Charmian, you don't drive," he added just as Alan drove up, tooting and grinning at Matt, to pick up his sister. Charmian dropped the cigarette in the gutter, stamped on it ineffectually, and got into the car and was borne off with a wave of her rosebud.

In the grounds of the Conservatorium the currawongs called, throwing notes into the air and catching them, keeping them afloat like balloons in a game at a child's party. It was a melancholy sound, though it shouldn't be. He was reminded of Emmy; it was the magic of the day that did it, the feeling that nothing existed but this exact moment. He longed for her to be there and share it with him. Her face, which now so often eluded him, was called up sweetly and distinctly: the freckles scattered across her cheeks like a trail of fuzzy stars, and the way she stared so earnestly into his eyes just before she kissed him.

Matt heard music from the street, where a busker in front of the health-food shop played on a flute, and it was so sharp and clear and elusive that it reminded him of Emmy all over again. After his unsuccessful attempt to write a song about Elijah, he'd never tried a song with words again, until one day, smitten with love for Emmy, he'd composed a piece of music on his guitar for her. But a bass guitar was the wrong instrument for her; it was too deep and rhythmic and plodding. This flute he heard now, it captured just the right quality. It was floating, elusive, enigmatic, and when you thought you'd worked out where the music was going, it seemed to take a deep breath and move off in an entirely different direction.

As Matt stood there, stricken by memories, Eliza came striding down the steps of the Con, hand in hand with the man he'd seen her with before—Kent, or Brent, or Trent. Talking avidly to him, laughing with amazement, full of the happiness that seemed to have come upon everyone that afternoon, she didn't see Matt and Mahalia waiting there for her under the trees.

* * *

"I need to tell you a secret," Emmy had whispered to him one day. She tore up a fig, all leather and gritty seeds. "I reckon I'm adopted, but they won't say."

Her evidence? She was an only child; and they were old when they had her; and married for years before that. She said she was not at all like them—she *had* to be adopted. She was defiant. She hated them because they wouldn't say. She had not asked, but she resented anyway. "It is up to them to tell me!" she hissed, standing up and going over to the edge of the river. And she jumped into the water. She came up gasping. That was when she said, "I wanted to see what it felt like."

Matt remembered what his mother had said about letting Mahalia get to know Emmy's parents, and he telephoned them and arranged to visit. Her mother sounded surprised, but suggested they come the next day.

Eliza helped him get Mahalia ready. She tried her out in a top she'd found at a thrift shop. It was a black T-shirt that said GIRLS KICK ASS in white letters. But it was a little on the large side still and didn't give the effect that Eliza thought was appropriate, so she settled for a pink shirt with buttons down the front.

"Do you take her to see her grandparents often?" she said.

"This is the first time," he said, "since Emmy went away. And before that, hardly ever. They didn't approve of us having her."

Eliza wiped away some grime from Mahalia's mouth and kissed her on the forehead.

"Why are you taking her to see them, then?"

"Well, because I want her to know the people she's related to." He thought of Otis's easygoing family. This visit with Emmy's parents mightn't work out, but he wanted to try. "She's got a whole life to live. It can't just be her and me all the time."

Eliza looked up at him quickly, then reached out for the brush and tidied up Mahalia's scanty hair.

"What are they like?"

Matt thought about it. "Ordinary. Fairly old. I never know what to say to them."

Eliza put a pink headband with a bow on top around Mahalia's head. "There, don't you look gorgeous!" she said, sitting back and gazing admiringly at Mahalia, who grinned back and clapped her hands together.

Matt and Mahalia took the bus to the brick suburb on the hills above the town. He remembered the neat brick house, the flower gardens with rock borders. He'd tripped over a garden border once when he went there late to climb in through Emmy's bedroom window. It had been the room of a little girl, with dolls and fake-flower arrangements and a frilly bedcover.

Emmy's mother met them at the door; she must have been watching for them. "Hello, Matt. Hello, Mahalia! What a big girl you are getting to be." Mahalia hid her face.

Emmy's father came down the side of the house, wiping his hands on a rag. He had retired, and one of his hobbies was tinkering with an old Austin he'd bought. He took Matt to see it, and Matt dutifully leaned inside the car to take a look, Mahalia on his hip. The car smelled of ancient leather and cracked varnish.

Inside the house, Matt sat in the living room with Mahalia on his knee. Through the hatch into the kitchen he saw Emmy's mother hesitate over the china cups and saucers and decide upon

Mahalia

the informality of mugs. She brought them in on a tray and placed them out on the wooden coffee table with coasters under them, and set down a plate with cream biscuits neatly arranged.

Mahalia was bored. She nuzzled against his shoulder and hid her face when she saw Emmy's mother looking at her. Matt would have liked to pick her up and show her objects around the room to amuse her but he didn't like to take the liberty in someone else's house. Besides, there were pictures of Emmy there, and that would have been awkward. No one had mentioned her at all.

Matt took a sip of tea and smiled at them both. "She's got teeth," he said, not able to think of anything else to say and putting his finger into Mahalia's mouth as if to demonstrate.

"She'd probably like to chew on something," said Emmy's mother, disappearing into the kitchen to get a crust of bread. Matt sat Mahalia on the floor while she ate it. Emmy's father ate a biscuit thoughtfully and said finally that he ought to be getting back to his car.

Emmy's mother seemed to relax a bit after he'd gone. She held out her arms to Mahalia; Mahalia grinned at her and blew her a bubble. Emmy's mother went out and came back with a teddy bear, small enough for Mahalia to hold easily. She took it and bit it immediately on the head.

Matt said that they ought to be getting back. They went out to say goodbye to Emmy's father, who offered to drive them back in the Austin. "The bus is fine," said Matt. "Anyway, I need to shop on the way home."

He surged along the road to the bus stop, feeling that he'd made an escape.

* * *

Mahalia began not sleeping at night.

She didn't seem to have anything really wrong with her. Perhaps her teeth—you could never tell. From here on it seemed to be all teething.

She would wake, and cry, and he'd change her and rock her and walk her, and she'd fall asleep, only to wake half an hour or fifteen minutes later. Her cries wrenched him awake, and each time it became harder and harder to get up to her.

It wasn't like the time when Matt couldn't sleep, the time he walked her through the streets, walking off his demons, the time when the black dog followed them. Now it was Mahalia who didn't want sleep, and Matt longed for it.

He would kill, he thought desperately, for sleep.

Eliza appeared, exhausted and rumpled, at his door one night, and said, "Do you think she's going to sleep, *ever?*" and then went off again to put her head under her pillow.

Sometimes Mahalia woke and didn't cry. She could pull herself upright using the bars of her crib now, and she stood there and called out to him until he answered and got up and took her into his bed. But she wanted to stay up and play. Their light was on and off all night.

During the day he was like a zombie, staring at nothing, not hearing what people said to him. He shopped for food in a daze. Sleep obsessed him. His body ached for it. When Mahalia slept, finally, sometimes during the afternoon, Matt lay on the bed and willed the world not to make a sound that might wake her. He hated any outside noise with a passion.

Though it was spring, the world threw cold, wet, windy mornings at them. With Mahalia awake and crying, Matt tore himself from the black warmth of the blanket covering his head and took her downstairs for breakfast. The house was dark and silent and damp, the worn linoleum gritty with dirt. Food was short. Matt discovered an egg in the door of the fridge and made some pancakes with powdered milk and the rest of a packet of whole-meal flour he found at the back of the cupboard. They were heavy and flat and chewy, but Mahalia picked them up in her fingers and ate them with great hunger and enjoyment. Her exclamations of delight did little to cheer him up in the grottiness of his morning.

Later, he picked up all the spare change he had lying around his room and decided to get the last ten bucks from his account to buy food for the rest of the week. He dressed Mahalia in a green nylon jacket with a hood; it was still too big and the long sleeves annoyed her. As he fastened the clips in the front, she tried to squirm out of it. "You want to stay dry, don't you?" he said. "Come on, you've gotta stay dry," roughly tugging it down and pulling the strings of the hood closed so tightly that her little face looked trapped.

The pleasure Mahalia had felt at her rubbery pancake breakfast had gone; she started to grizzle as he strapped her into the stroller and continued to whine as they went out the door and down the street toward town. Wind blew a light spray of raindrops across their faces; Matt tried to shut his ears to her cries by concentrating on everything else around him. A car with a faulty muffler burbled along the street; a bicycle whizzed past, its wheels spraying water. Matt put his head down against the rain and watched his feet pound the dirty footpath, and Mahalia's pathetic cries became a monotonous complaint inside his head, reminding him of his deficiencies as a father. They had rotten food and lived in a grotty old place. He had to wheel her out through wind and rain to flatten his bank account in order to eat. Matt's foot slipped on a dog turd. He scraped the soles of his sneakers off on the wet gutter, but the stench followed him down the street. A red apple with several bites taken from it lay in his path and he kicked it aside. The footpath ended at a laneway and Matt jolted the stroller down into the roadway so violently that Mahalia began to wail.

"Shut up, Mahalia! Give us a break!" Matt gripped the stroller and the handles bit into his fingers. He lurched the stroller to one side and shook it.

Mahalia was crying softly now, a pitiful sound, lonely and bewildered. Matt knelt down in front of her and stared into her face with dismay. A line of clear snot ran from her nose onto her upper lip. Her face was damp from tears and the rain; he wiped it gently with his sleeve.

Mahalia stopped crying and stared into his face. Her eyes were round and dark and steady. *We're in this together,* her look said.

"Yeah, mate," he said quietly. "Let's get this shopping out of the way."

Virginia looked after Mahalia one night, so that Matt could get some sleep. She slept in his room, so that Mahalia would have the familiarity of her own place.

Matt crawled into Virginia's bed and conked out.

He awoke in the night when he heard Mahalia's voice, wakeful and happy, talking to Virginia, babbling, imitating the sounds Virginia made, having a conversation with her. He went back to sleep.

In the morning Virginia staggered into the kitchen with a rueful expression. "Boy, that kid can stay up. I think we should try and change her sleeping pattern or something. She just doesn't want to sleep at night, that's all. Just where does she get her energy from? That's what I want to know."

And yet there were times on balmy nights when the house was still and Mahalia slept solidly and certainly, when Matt felt that the house bellied out and contained them all in a firm, floating globe.

He thought of the way his hands would cup Emmy's pregnant belly in sleep. It was a natural object: a pear, an egg, a drop of water grown heavy and about to fall. It was architectural: a vault, a dome, a container filled with promise.

So the old shop held them and rocked them. He imagined the walls curving outward, the building becoming so globular and light that it could float. When the wind blew, it rocked and groaned and stretched its timbers like a ship at sea. He would see it from outside at night, the lights shining out like beacons. Inside it was filled with light and shadows, and Eliza's purposeful footsteps, and Mahalia's soft, milky breath.

Eliza watched him. He could feel it. She watched him through the back door as he hung out Mahalia's clothes on the line, sitting at the kitchen table, her feet on the rungs of a chair next to her, her hand stilled in the act of pulling back the heavy weight of hair. She turned her head away at his approach and got to her feet, disappearing up the stairs.

"Do you want to take Mahalia up to the swings?" she said one day, her head in the fridge, rummaging for food.

"Okay."

The park was at the end of a narrow street near their place. Mahalia kicked her legs eagerly and rocked the stroller back and forth as they went. She had grown out of the sun hat Eliza had originally found for her, and now she had another one, ferreted out at St. Vinnie's by Matt this time. It was securely held by a tie under her chin: he had learned a thing or two about buying clothes for a baby by now.

They walked down the street slowly, enjoying the rambling country feel of the place. Inhabited almost entirely by people like themselves, it was a place where untidy lives were lived temporarily and happily.

The timber houses had ancient, flaking paint and stood high off the ground to keep out of floods, for the river was close by. They'd been filled in underneath just anyhow with old doors and windows, to use the extra space. For months after a flood the underneath of the house would stink of river mud. The gardens surrounding all the houses were wild and there were no fences between them.

Eliza paused between two of the houses where there was a path leading into the garden. "Do you want to come in and look?"

"I don't know," said Matt. "Wouldn't it be intruding?"

"They won't mind." Eliza shook her head and smiled at Matt's hesitation. She unstrapped Mahalia from the stroller and carried her up the tangled path, ducking her head to avoid branches.

"Permaculture, right?" said Matt.

Everything grew in this garden, all mixed together. Paths rambled round beds filled with flowers and herbs and vegetables, all heavily mulched with straw. There were fruit trees growing amongst the vegetables, citrus and mangoes and papaw, and rainforest trees as well. Eliza bent down to pick a cherry tomato from a bush, and she squeezed the juice into Mahalia's mouth.

"Yum, eh, Mahalia?" She turned her head to say to Matt, "I used to live here—for a while."

"It's like the Garden of Eden," said Matt. "Why did you leave?"

Eliza grimaced. "*Luurve*," she said in an exaggerated way, as if that explained everything. "I mean, I was in love here. It didn't work out."

"Aren't you afraid—"

He was about to say, *of running into him here*. But she understood, without him needing to finish the sentence.

"He left too."

"Oh." Matt found himself not wanting to run into an old love of Eliza's, even if it *was* over.

Eliza smiled and waved to some people in the garden behind the house next door, which was a continuation of the garden they were in, and led Matt around the house and out onto the street again. The park was only a short stroll away now.

They were the only ones that day in the dappled park. Mahalia was still too small to sit on a swing by herself, so Matt took a seat and held her on his lap, pushing it gently forward and back with his feet. Mahalia laughed, and urged him forward with pushing movements of her body. It surprised him how strong she could be. She willed things; knew what she wanted to do.

"I'll probably feel sick in a while," he said. "I've never been able to take swings."

"Oh, then I'll take over," said Eliza. "Just say when you'd like me to take her."

She sat on the swing next to them, her long legs pushing her higher with each arc, till Matt thought she might go right over the top of the swing. It made him dizzy to watch.

Emmy had always swung like that too.

Eliza finally stopped and came to take Mahalia on the swing with her. She held the baby firmly across the chest with one arm and with the other held the chain of the swing. Higher and higher they went, till Matt feared for Mahalia's safety, but she was squealing with pleasure.

"What is it with girls and swings? And girls and horses for that matter?" he said when Eliza finally touched ground and propelled a laughing Mahalia back into his arms.

"Oh well, if you don't know that . . . ," said Eliza. She was panting, and beads of sweat stood out on her upper lip. She licked them away.

Next they went on a whirly thing, a flat disc of metal that someone had to push, then leap onto at the last moment as the whole thing spun recklessly around like a top. Eliza did the pushing, and Matt sat in the middle and held on to the bar with Mahalia in his arms, but he was dizzy far sooner than either of them were. When it had slowed down enough, they staggered away and collapsed together in a heap on the grass.

Eliza challenged him to an arm wrestle. Although she was strong, he could have won if he'd made the effort, but then something in him simply gave out and his arm collapsed onto the ground. Perhaps it was her lion's eyes, their slight concentration toward the middle of her face that did it. They never left his, willing him to defeat.

When they arrived back, Matt took Mahalia to have a bath. She was big enough to sit in a proper tub now, if he stayed beside her and propped her up. She loved to suck on the washcloth, pushing her face into it the way a dog wrestles with a bone.

They were nearly finished when Eliza came to the door of the bathroom. "You've got a visitor," she said.

Matt wrapped Mahalia in a towel and went downstairs. Mahalia was naked and pink, and sucked on her rubber duck. She clung harder to Matt when she saw the stranger there.

"I hope you don't mind me calling in," said Emmy's mother, "but you said I could, and you didn't say whether you had a phone." She looked anxious.

Matt came forward with a smile. He'd never been sure how to address Emmy's mother, so he didn't call her anything. "Would you like to come in?"

He took her to the kitchen, where Eliza was making pizzas. Matt introduced them, hesitating over Emmy's mother's name, *Mrs. Wood*. He wasn't used to calling people "Mrs." He called all his mother's friends by their first name.

"Would you like a cup of tea?" asked Eliza. "It's no trouble!" she added brightly.

"No, thank you. I'm only staying a moment." Matt offered Mrs. Wood a chair and she sat down, smiling quickly up at him.

She sat awkwardly opposite Matt at the table. Mahalia sucked on her rubber duck and looked at her grandmother gravely, overtaken by Matt's serious mood.

"I wondered . . . ," said Emmy's mother, ". . . I came to see if Mahalia could visit us sometime. On her own. She could stay the night, if you liked."

Matt hadn't expected this. He felt dismayed. He hadn't minded visiting them, but this was unexpected. He looked toward Eliza, but her back was turned to him; she was tactfully rolling out pizza dough at the counter near the sink.

"I'd rather she didn't stay overnight," he said. "She's not used to being without me." He frowned, thinking about it, trying to sort out his feelings, weighing them against what he supposed was reasonable. The truth of the matter was that the thought of Mahalia going somewhere without him made him panic.

Mahalia

"But I suppose you could take her for a few hours if you liked," he said. He thought he could live with that. "She's at the stage where she's scared of strangers, though, and . . . she doesn't know you very well."

Emmy's mother reached her hand across the table toward Mahalia, who turned her face and hid it against Matt's shoulder. "If she comes to visit us, she'll soon get to know us," said Emmy's mother. "Won't you?" she added, smiling at Mahalia, who had turned to stare at her with wide eyes.

"Well, I suppose it would be all right—just for a short time," said Matt.

"Would later this week do—Friday?"

"Okay." Matt felt like a traitor, for Mahalia was sitting on his lap, warm in her rough towel, trusting and innocent.

"All right, then. I'll pick her up. Would ten in the morning suit you?"

Matt nodded.

Emmy's mother got to her feet and said goodbye to Eliza, and Matt walked her to the front door. Afterward, he took Mahalia upstairs to dress her and, with a heavy heart, carried her back down to the kitchen, where Eliza was putting the toppings on her pizzas.

Eliza said nothing to Matt about the visit, but for Mahalia's benefit, looking into the baby's face and smiling, she named the ingredients aloud as she placed them on the dough. ". . . some tomatoes," she said, "some capsicum, some mozzarella cheese, and"—said with a flourish—"a little bit of salami for happiness!"

Matt tried to see some connection between Emmy with her wild ways and slight, slim body and the plump, staid woman who'd sat in his kitchen; but he couldn't. Maybe Emmy *was* adopted, as she'd suspected.

Then again, Matt couldn't see any similarity between himself and his own father either. His father hadn't disclaimed his parentage of Matt, but had never wanted to be a father to him. If Emmy had been adopted, Matt felt his father had un-adopted him.

Matt's father had three cacti on his windowsill: a hairy one, a small one like a button, and a double-headed one.

He put them where they would get the most sun. He'd been told cacti need at least four hours of sunshine a day in order to flower. Matt wasn't there long enough to see that happen.

Matt had known his father for exactly a week.

At least, that was the way he thought of it, for it was the total time they spent together.

When he was fourteen, he'd started asking about his father again. He hadn't asked since he was five. This time his mother arranged for them to meet.

On the way down the coast in the train, Matt looked out at the country rolling by and wondered why his mother had never taken him to meet his father on one of their almost annual trips to Sydney to see her friends. He wondered if he should have a name badge so his father would recognize him.

He was surprised by his father's soft American accent. His mother hadn't told him about that. His mother hadn't told him much at all, mainly because she felt that it was his father's business to tell him. But his father wasn't good at doing that. Anything Matt knew he had to gather for himself.

His father was neat. That and his accent were the most

noticeable things about him. He was smaller than Matt too, and even though he wasn't very old his hair was gray. He wasn't a suit wearer, he didn't have to be because he taught at a university, but he wore neat pressed trousers and neatly ironed shirts, with small blue checks mostly. He didn't do his own ironing; he paid someone else to do it.

He drove a small flashy car—a Saab, but an old one. The plush seats and the swift clean handling of the car through the city streets was unlike the bumpy progress of the old cars along dirt roads that Matt was used to, and he felt alien. *I hate cars*, Matt told himself. *I'll never drive a car, especially not one like this.*

His father's voice was so soft it made Matt feel loud. He felt loud and awkward and too tall next to his neat, small father. Matt swallowed his loud, Australian-accented voice in shame and embarrassment.

His father worked a lot in his study, marking papers and preparing classes; even though Matt was on school holidays, the university didn't seem to be. So Matt crept around the flat or stayed in his room, trying not to make too much noise.

The room Matt stayed in was blue, with a neatly made bed and framed pictures on the walls. He was the loneliest he'd ever been in that room. He lay on the bed and ticked off in his mind the days he was to stay.

Everything in the kitchen had its place. His father cooked neat meals and was as fastidious as a cat. The breakfast toast had crumbs so dry they stuck in Matt's throat.

They had absolutely nothing to say to each other. Because his father was an academic, learning stuff from books was his thing.

He'd asked Matt about school, and Matt had answered politely, hesitantly, but school wasn't really *his* thing, and it showed.

Matt remembered sitting next to him in a coffee shop in Glebe, a place full of smart city people. His father read the Saturday papers. He smiled at Matt when he turned the page, and slipped him some money to go off and get something of his own to read. Matt bought a copy of *Modern Guitarist*, and when he came back with it, his father looked at the cover and raised an eyebrow. "Do you play?" he asked, and Matt nodded. "That's great!" said his father, nodding. Then he went back to his paper, not in an unfriendly way, Matt thought, but because he couldn't think of anything else to say. And neither could Matt.

Matt had wished he'd brought his guitar, so at least he could show his father he could do *something*. His irrational desire to win this man's approval confused him and left him resentful and even more determined not to sit in a room all his life *reading books and pushing pens*, as he put it to himself.

And when Matt got home, the thing he most wanted to ask his mother (but didn't, because he feared hurting her feelings) was *why* and *how* they had ever got together long enough to have him.

At this stage of his life Matt felt there should enter an old carpenter or stonemason or some sort of positive male role model who would apprentice him and help him make something of himself.

But such a person wasn't going to materialize. As Matt walked the streets of Lismore, pushing the stroller in front of him, going into shops to search out the scrappy food that kept them alive, he saw only people like himself, people getting by and making do. But life had a tenacious streak, and optimism always asserted itself.

"Hey, you've got a beautiful baby!" said a woman in an overcoat with matted orange fur like a teddy bear that had been loved too much. It wasn't cold, but she wore a coat anyway, and with her hands in her pockets, she fanned the flaps at the front of the coat as she walked.

That made Matt smile. He gave a skip and ran the stroller extra fast, and Mahalia clutched the side of the stroller and urged it forward with her body, as if she were riding a horse.

He bathed Mahalia, dressed her neatly for another visit to Emmy's parents, packed a bag: some diapers and spare clothes and her plastic drinking cup with the lid and two teddy bears and a rattle that Charmian had given her.

Emmy's parents had put a baby car seat in the back of their car, and as Matt leaned inside and plopped her onto the cozy wool seat cover, Mahalia laughed and thought it was a game. He clicked her into the seat belt and tickled her under the arms. But when he stepped back and closed the door, she realized that she was being abandoned; she squealed with rage and pushed her chest forward, puffing it up against the restraining belt. She held out her arms to him and cried, and Matt, at the last moment, raced round to the other side of the car and wrenched open the back door.

"You don't mind if I come?" he said. Emmy's mother's face was reflected in the rearview mirror. He couldn't make out her expression but he flashed her a smile. His hand rested comfortingly on the top of Mahalia's head. "I don't think she's ready to go by herself yet."

It seemed a long visit. In between the ritual of morning tea and lunch, they sat and watched Mahalia's antics and talked awkwardly about her. There wasn't a lot to say.

Mahalia could pull herself up by holding on to a piece of furniture, and she stood clutching the sofa and beating her hand proudly against the seat. She always knew when she had achieved something and liked other people to notice it too.

At lunch, she picked up her food delicately between her index finger and thumb and put it fastidiously in her mouth and chewed with great enjoyment. She seemed to sense that they were visitors, for she didn't throw things on the floor for Matt to pick up endlessly as she did at home.

Mahalia

She sat for ages on the living-room floor and put clothespins into a tin and then took them out again, seeming never to tire of it, looking up and laughing at Matt and at Emmy's mother every so often to show them she knew how clever she was.

They sat and watched her, embarrassed and dismayed by the possibility of conversation. Finally Matt thought that perhaps he could decently end the visit, and he offered to catch a bus back, but Emmy's mother insisted that she drive them, and Mahalia sang all the way home.

If sometimes Matt experienced his life as robust and full and expectant, there were other times when all seemed to be fragility. Then the weathered boards of the old shop appeared as thin and tenuous as his life. There was a flimsiness to it; it could be torn down in an instant. At these times Matt felt vulnerable, lay curled on his bed trying not to think how he could manage it all, and was tugged reluctantly back to the world by Mahalia's wail as she woke.

There were days without money that could stretch into weeks. When the rent and power bills were due, no one in the house had any spare cash. Eliza ate when she went to her coffee-shop job, and it didn't seem to matter to Virginia whether she ate or not; her thin body seemed to be able to exist without the benefit of food, but Matt always needed to eat, and he wouldn't let Mahalia go without.

The times when he and Elijah used to go bush and live off the land had been good training for him. There wasn't much that Matt didn't regard as food. He and Elijah had eaten hairy mussels from the creek that had tasted of mud, and old catfish so oily and strong-tasting that he had almost gagged on them. They'd munched on lilly-pilly fruits, some as delicious as apples and others with a taste like eucalyptus oil. If worse came to worst, Matt thought, he'd head into the bush and kill something. He wouldn't ask his mother for help; he always let on that everything was fine.

There was a tangled garden that beckoned to him as he walked down a back lane near their house each day, where the trees were full of mandarins and oranges and lemons. They lay on the ground, ignored and abandoned, which led him to believe that no one picked them or wanted them. The place seemed deserted. Matt's mouth tingled at the thought of all that sweet juicy fruit going to waste. One day he went round the front of the house and opened the rusty gate, unstrapped Mahalia from her stroller, and went up the three splintered wooden steps to the front door.

No one answered his knock, though the front windows were wide open. Old cotton curtains hung limply behind them; there was no movement from inside the house. Matt went round the back and the fruit was there for the taking. He sat Mahalia under the tree and, with his heart racing, started picking. Even after he'd filled the canvas shopping bag he always wore over his shoulder, no impression had been made on the glut of fruit on the trees.

Matt returned a few days later, then again, and again, and never saw a soul, and the fruit was all the sweeter for having been bestowed on him like that.

It was time, Matt thought, to be serious about getting a job. He asked Eliza to cut his hair.

Her professionalism showed. She was a bold and decisive

cutter of hair. None of that tentative lifting and combing, a few strands off here and there the way some people did. Her hair-cutting was as assertive as her walk, as intended as the songs she sang. In no time at all Matt's hair was in a neat straight bob. He pushed it behind his ears and examined himself in the mirror.

"It makes you look younger."

"Does it?" Matt was anxious. "Too young?"

"Not *too* young. Really, though, it looks good."

Virginia walked through the room and whistled. "What do you think, Mahalia, doesn't he look great?"

Matt smiled at himself in the mirror. He was clean-cut. He looked fine.

Matt asked Charmian to baby-sit each morning and went, full of hope and fear, to places where machinery ground and sparked and men in overalls walked purposefully back and forth with bits of metal and spare parts. Matt had a sense that something myste-rious and hidden was taking place there; if only he could gain an entry to that secret world of work, everything would be all right for him and Mahalia.

He went to sandwich bars and retail outlets. There was nothing. No one wanted him—no one but Mahalia, it seemed, who squealed with pleasure each day when he appeared at Charmian's back door.

Every day he hauled out his neatest clothes.

Who are you trying to fool? he asked himself after his twenty-eighth rejection. He felt humiliated; it was harder and harder each time to walk up to a place. Some people were friendly, but couldn't help him—"No, mate, no, sorry, we've got all the people we need!"—while others looked him over suspiciously, or simply had no time for him.

"I reckon if it's gonna happen, it'll happen," said Virginia, making him a coffee in the kitchen on the afternoon when he'd more or less given up.

"Yeah? What kind of talk is that from you?"

"You're right. I'm bullshittin'. Just tryin' to make you feel better." Virginia laughed with a shamed face, showing her teeth. She pulled her cap down over her eyes and looked at him bashfully. "Maybe when Mahalia's older. You could go to TAFE or somethin'. Don't they have someone down at Centrelink to help single parents get jobs?"

In the dim light in the kitchen, mosquitoes had already started hovering, anticipating nightfall. They nudged his feet and he ignored their prickling until he remembered the possibility of Ross River fever and slapped them away. He got up to light a coil, and when the smoke from the coil wound past her, Mahalia tried to catch it.

Early one cool morning, Matt searched for Eliza at the Con, up and down stairs, following the blue carpet worn on the treads. There was a smell in his nostrils of cool, clean early morning. Dim light, filtered by camphor-laurel trees, dappled the corridors. Somewhere a man warbled like Tarzan, a primitive sound, made for fun. The place seemed even more silent when he'd finished.

Matt hurried, holding Mahalia close to his chest. She was silent and awestruck by his urgency. Her mouth gaped like a little fish's.

He found Eliza in a classroom where students were gathering. She looked around at his approach.

"Can you take Mahalia? I've been offered a job. They want me to start right now!"

"Well, I've got to be here today!" But she took Mahalia when he handed her over.

"She'll be no trouble. Look, I've left her stroller outside, and there's some diapers in a bag in the back of it. She'll eat anything—just give her something to drink and a mouthful of your lunch."

"Matt!"

"Please. It just came up, and I wasn't even looking—I had Mahalia with me. At that vego café down the street. Kitchen hand. Someone just left and they want someone fast. If you get time later, you can drop her at Charmian's."

"I don't even know Charmian!"

Matt was already out the door.

Matt worked all day, and he found that you could *sweat* from simply slicing vegetables and juicing oranges and washing up, if you did it hard enough and fast enough and long enough. When they needed more people serving on the tables, he wiped his face with his apron and went out and took orders. And after lunch it only slowed down a little: there was the washing up and more slicing and grating to make cakes for the next day. There were no labor-saving devices, no slicers or food processors or dishwashing machines.

At five o'clock he was whacked, but he hurried home to Mahalia.

"How was she?" he asked breathlessly, arriving in the kitchen, where Eliza was setting out food on the tray of her high chair. Mahalia greeted him with a squeal and a wave of her arm.

Eliza gave him a surly look. "Okay. I had to come home from the Con, though, and miss a whole day's classes."

"You could've sat her beside you on the floor."

"Yeah. Right. And *you* could've sat her on the floor of the café while you worked. She needs *attention*, Matt, you know that. She kept wanting me to pick her up and talk to her. She wanted food all the time. Her diaper needed changing."

Matt stared at Eliza. "You're angry at me."

"You just didn't think."

"But hey, I needed this job. I had to take it straightaway or someone else would have. I'll get someone else for tomorrow."

She shot him a look and stomped off up the stairs.

He could hear her running a shower, but tonight no songs came belting through the house. Matt sat down next to Mahalia and helped her with her meal. She babbled her baby talk and he replied to her, but in a subdued way, because he was so tired, and sad, too, in a way he couldn't fathom. He'd been working so fast and furiously he'd had no time to think of her, but now that they were together, he was aware that he had missed her. What had she done today?

He lifted her out of her high chair and went out and watered Eliza's herbs, holding Mahalia on one hip as he worked. Someone came and stood at his elbow. "Anyway," he said, "thanks, Eliza, for doing that for me today."

He looked down at her sideways, and she smiled reluctantly before walking back into the house.

Matt sliced and shredded. Fast. And faster. He couldn't go fast enough. He dropped food on the floor. Broke a plate.

The café buzzed at him through the bead curtain. It was only eleven o'clock. A fly hovered around his face and he waved it away. He pressed oranges onto a juicer. Liquid dripped from the cutting board. He slid on the wet floor, his shoes making a muddy mark, righted himself like a skier, but pain shot down his back.

He mopped the floor.

He sweated into the dishwater, wiped his forehead, and then went out to take more orders.

At last, in the middle of the lunchtime rush, Matt's knife slipped and he cut his hand, right in the fleshy ball below his thumb. A gash, sudden and deep, welled blood, and he was thrown a tea towel. "Wrap it tight."

There were no bandages in the first-aid box.

Matt worked on, and the tea towel showed bright blotches, like flowers.

After work he went to pick up Mahalia from Charmian's. "She been fussing all day. Wanting 'er dad. What's wrong with your hand?"

"I cut it. Thanks, Charmian. Look . . ." Matt wrestled some money from his pocket with his good hand, but Charmian waved it away. "No. No need to pay me. But, Matt, I can't do this all the time. And I've got to go away tomorrow. Down to Kempsey, me old auntie's died. I'll be away awhile. Month or so, prob'ly."

Matt thanked her again and took Mahalia and his hand home. His hand felt like that to him, something he was carting around separate to himself.

When he got home, he unwrapped it gingerly and showed it to Eliza. "You'd better take that to the hospital. Looks like it needs stitches to me." She held out her arms for Mahalia, who cried at being separated again from Matt so soon. Exhausted, he spent some of his precious pay on a taxi.

At the hospital Matt bought a cold can of Coke from a machine and alternately sipped it and pressed it onto his cut through the cloth, hoping the cold would give relief. His hand throbbed and he sat and watched as people came and went. He felt faint from lack of food. He'd found there is no time to eat when you work at a café.

A young man was brought in with a motorcycle injury. Another came in, raving, saying his teeth were hurting. He was told to wait, and he sat, telling imaginary people to *shut the hell up*. He jumped up and went outside; Matt saw him pacing with a cigarette, gesturing to the invisible people who haunted him. Then he stormed in and went to the desk again, muttering to himself and glaring at the people waiting in the room.

At last it was Matt's turn.

"When did this happen?" said the doctor.

"About twelve-thirty."

"It needs stitches. You should have come in earlier."

Matt winced as the doctor cleaned it.

"Is this a work injury?"

"No," said Matt. "I did it at home."

The doctor looked unconvinced. Matt thought of the cash the café owner had given him. There'd be no record of his working— no workers' compensation. It was lousy money. But enough. Enough to do the work again the next day.

His hand took seven stitches.

Mahalia

* * *

At home he lay in bed in the dark and listened to Mahalia cry while his hand throbbed. He got up and tried to settle her a couple of times. The throb and the crying seemed to be assaulting him from all sides.

Matt lay with his eyes closed and listened to Mahalia's feeble cries. He could see that she was tired too, but she couldn't settle. A tear ran down the side of his face. It was a tear of exhaustion and self-pity and remorse. He longed for Emmy to be there. *I'm sorry*, he said to her in his head. *I'm sorry*.

Mahalia's cries continued, more urgently now. She was trying to make him take notice of her.

"I hate you, Mahalia," he said softly to himself, without expression. He listened to the words without interest. It was as though someone other than himself was saying them.

The cries continued. He put on the light and looked down into her crib as if she were an object unknown to him: not his; not a person. He bent down and picked her up wearily, but the wailing continued. He changed her diaper, offered her a bottle, but she turned her head away. He put her into the bed beside him and looked into her face.

What he said was experimental, to see how the words sounded out loud: "I hate you, Mahalia."

Said to her face like that, they were a transgression, a blasphemy. He was saying the unthinkable.

But he'd said them too softly.

Say them louder. And with meaning.

"I hate you, Mahalia. Everything's hard because of you."

* * *

Just before Matt had left school they'd had a substitute teacher for history one day. He was Danish or Swedish or something. And he was *crazy!* the class thought. *Crazy!* He raved on about *the optimistic carp*. He said the Japanese liked carp because they were so optimistic, swimming up rivers and up waterfalls, struggling against the odds. He talked about it for almost the entire lesson!

They laughed at him, nearly laughed themselves sick. "He's a lunatic!" they told each other as they rushed out for lunch. "Crazy! Off the planet!"

Matt told his mother.

"Do carp do that?" she said, and frowned. "Are you sure he didn't mean trout, or salmon?"

"No. Carp," Matt told her.

And she said, "That's nice. I like the idea of an optimistic carp."

Matt did too, when he thought about it. He'd thought the teacher was crazy, but that lesson was the only thing Matt remembered about school.

Matt woke late with his hand still throbbing and Mahalia apparently a bit off-color. He decided not to keep at the job, and hated himself for being weak, for giving up too easily, for not being able to hack it.

He needn't have agonized. When he turned up at the café with Mahalia in the stroller to say he couldn't make it, he discovered someone else working in the kitchen anyway: the person he'd taken over from, who'd come back from wherever it was he'd gone. It turned out the job had been only temporary, only he hadn't been told.

Mahalia

Matt went past the pawnshop and looked in the window. He'd been hoping to earn a bit of cash to get his guitar back, but knew in his heart that it would have taken second place to all the other things he and Mahalia needed money for anyway. He reckoned he could kiss BLUES IS THE MUSIC THAT HEALS goodbye.

Matt walked past a man he'd seen many times, who was also always wheeling a baby around town in a stroller. He was black but not a Koori, a West Indian perhaps. He and his child both had hair plaited in a multitude of tiny braids with beads on them. He and Matt had noticed each other often, Matt knew, but in a surreptitious way. Today they caught each other's eye.

The man saw Matt looking at him. He grinned at Matt and said, "That's a beautiful baby you've got there!"

"Thank you," said Matt. "You too!"

A little way farther on, Matt stopped the stroller and knelt down in front of Mahalia, looking into her face. "Hey, Mahalia, hey," he said softly and happily. "Looks like you've got your old man back, ay?"

They went home down the laneway of the house that had the oranges and the mandarins. Matt jumped over the fence, bold now, and he and Mahalia ate mandarins directly under the tree, their faces held up to the spring sunshine.

12

The back door was always open and it seemed to have always been summer. Matt sweated even at night, lying sleepless in the heat, slapping at mosquitoes. But there were compensations. Scents wafted from other people's yards, and there was a mango tree over the back with heavy clusters of white flowers. It was a magical time when miracles seemed bound to happen.

The front door, too, was left open most of the day now. Matt put up a wooden barricade so that Mahalia couldn't crawl out onto the street. She used it to pull herself up and stood at the barricade waving to passersby. People stopped to talk to her, and she charmed them with her smile and the conversations she carried on in her own language.

One night when Eliza was out somewhere, Matt and Virginia went down to the pub on the corner for a good feed. They sat out in the beer garden and Matt was content to let Virginia rave on to him, with the fairy lights in the trees and the sound of the recorded music and the voices and laughter, until Mahalia fell asleep under his feet with her bottom in the air.

Then he wasn't sorry either to pick her up and sling her, still sleeping, against his shoulder, and walk the short distance home with Virginia. He put Mahalia into her crib and washed some of her clothes by hand and hung them on the veranda outside his room. With his belly still pleasantly full of steak and onions and mashed potatoes, he lay down on his bed and wrote to Emmy.

We are living in a house with nice people, he said. *Mahalia is crawling like anything and she can pull herself up if she hangs on to something. She can move about by holding on to bits of furniture. I reckon she'll be walking soon.*

But the contentment that allowed him to begin a letter to Emmy left him as soon as he wrote those words, for they made him realize how much of Mahalia she was missing out on. He crumpled up the piece of paper and began again, a *nothing* letter, he thought, as he folded it into an envelope and addressed it.

Then the feeling of longing to see Emmy again came upon him suddenly, as it always did. It lay treacherously in wait, coming when he least expected it, at times when he was feeling halfway happy and content with his life. It was a feeling of such loss and longing that it was sweet, in the way revenge is meant to be sweet, and he wallowed in it, and let memories of her fill his head.

Late that night, when all the world was quiet and Matt still hadn't fallen asleep, he got out of bed and went onto the balcony, the summery air on his face. He stood and gazed through the latticework into the street.

The streetlight hung golden, beset by fluttering moths. The silence was broken by a car squealing past, and the yap of a dog. The wind chimes tinkled, slow and insistent, gathering in the wind to an excited rattle.

Matt imagined that the house had stored sounds during the day, to release them into his mind in the dead of night. He imagined he heard the sound of Eliza singing, slow and throaty, or Virginia's laugh, turning involuntarily into a cough. Mahalia's voice was there too, her *da . . . da*, a wondering sound at the magic of her own language.

He stood gazing and remembering till he forgot himself with delight, to be brought back by the sound of Mahalia waking.

On Christmas Day, Matt went up to his mother's. She had invited people over as usual and made it into a real celebration, with wonderful food and lots of music.

Emmy had sent a present for Mahalia to his mother's address. Matt didn't feel celebratory when he helped Mahalia open it. It was a plush horse, and of course, she loved it. He hadn't written to Emmy of the horses down the road and his letter hadn't mentioned any of the important stuff of their everyday lives, but she'd picked just the right thing.

There was a note for Matt in with the present. *I'm thinking of you both heaps*, it said.

Matt had taken it outside to read, and he crumpled it quickly and shoved it deep inside the compost heap.

Some mornings Matt slept so heavily that almost nothing could wake him except Mahalia. He was wired for the sound of her voice; sometimes a cough in the night could wake him, and he would lie there long after she'd gone back to sleep, floating half-awake in the darkness.

Eliza's friend from the Conservatorium, whose name Matt finally got into his head was Kent, came to visit, and Eliza took him to her room, where Matt heard the maddening murmur of their voices for hours, and too much laughter. Kent finally left before midnight but was back again the next day. He stopped on his way through the house to listen to Matt and Otis jamming (Matt still on Alan's old *heap of shit,* as Otis affectionately liked to call it) in the front room. "Hey, you boys aren't bad," he said. "You should do something with your music. Get a band together or something."

Otis grinned and dismissed the idea. "Yeah, man. As if."

"Neither of you plays bass, do you?" said Kent. "Our player's leaving in a month or so."

"He does," said Otis, nodding toward Matt. "But his guitar's out of action for a while."

"Well, if it gets into action, think about it," said Kent, looking into Matt's eyes as if he meant it. His eyes were dark and frank and kind; he had a maturity about him that made Matt feel too young. Unhappily, Matt could too easily see why Eliza wanted to spend time with him. The planes of his face, which his shaved head accentuated, his muscular body, and his careless confidence showed already the kind of man he'd matured into. There was nothing fuzzy or unformed about him at all. Matt fiddled with the tuning of the crap guitar so as to avoid blushing. *Him,* in a band, when it was Otis who was the real musician.

Mahalia had been standing at the barricade to the street and wailed when Eliza and Kent stepped over it on their way out.

Eliza turned and bent down to her face and kissed her. "See you later, honey bun!"

Matt's mother had given Mahalia a book for Christmas. It was called *On the Way to the Barn* and it was full of farm animals. She soon learned to snort like a pig and moo like a cow. She liked the horse the best, and she patted it, the way she patted the horses in the paddock up the road.

Eliza liked to read it to her. She bundled Mahalia up into her arms and carried her off to her room and into her bed. Matt came to the door one night and stood there uncertainly until Eliza patted the bed on the other side of her, inviting him to join them.

Matt couldn't help but be aware of Eliza beside him. He smelled faintly her perspiration from the hot day. It wasn't an unpleasant odor. He closed his eyes and listened.

"What kind of noises can you make today? Can you moo like a cow, grunt like a pig?" Mahalia and Eliza mooed and grunted. With his eyes closed, the voices seemed strange, as if they were coming to him a long way through a tunnel. Finally they faded, and Matt slept.

"I'll read *you* a story," Eliza told him one night when Mahalia was asleep.

They lay on her bed together, at a safe distance.

"My mum used to do this," said Matt. "Read to me."

Eliza smiled to herself and began.

She read him a story from her childhood. It was called *The Day Boy and the Night Girl*, and it was about two children who were raised by a witch, the boy never to see the night, and the girl never knowing what the day was. The boy was never allowed up after sunset and the girl was kept in an underground room and slept in the day, while at night her only light was a dim lamp hanging from the ceiling.

One night, when she was grown-up, she found her way outside

and thought that it was daylight (for she had heard of it) because the moon was so bright. And the boy, now grown also, defied the witch and stayed out after dark, but he was terrified of it. They met, and helped each other to escape the witch, and taught each other to live at the other time of day.

Eliza finished reading and they lay there, side by side, still not touching. It seemed that the magic and mystery of the story had entered their world. A breeze came through the window, carrying sounds from the house behind them. A child called, "Mum? Can I sleep outside tonight? In my tent?"

"I think I'm a night boy," said Matt. "I love the night. I think it's beautiful."

"Then I'm a day girl," said Eliza. "I love sunshine. It helps my herbs to grow."

Matt lay stretched out on her bed, his hands behind his head. He smiled to himself. He felt comfortable, and at peace.

"How about telling *me* a story?" said Eliza. She rolled over onto her side, her head propped on one elbow.

"All right," said Matt. "I'll tell you the story of how Mahalia got her name."

When Matt had gone to stay with his father for the first time (the only time!), he'd asked himself *why* and *how*. How come his mother, a person who got her fingernails grubby with earth, who had built her own improvised house, who said, "Lipstick rots your brain," came to be with a man whose toaster wasn't sullied with one single crumb (or not for long).

But there was a day in that long week, a day when both of them had lost the will to go out and pretend to have a good time with each other, when his father said, "You tell me you're inter-ested in blues, listen to this. It's not blues. It's gospel."

And his father had put on a record of a woman singing, and the sound poured into Matt's eardrums and scratched them and filled them with treacle all at once. It was high and ecstatic music. It *swung* with feeling. It was the most joyful sound Matt had ever heard.

When it had finished, Matt's father sat quietly, and the silence that filled the room was different from any silence that Matt had ever experienced, and there was such a look on his father's face. It was a look that Matt had forgotten until now, but that suddenly all added up. It was a look of passion, and it made him alive and irresistible.

"That was Mahalia Jackson," his father said. "Always remem-ber that name."

And he said the name in a whoop of joy: "MA–HA–LI–A. MA–HA–LI–A!"

When Matt told Eliza the story of his visit, and how his father had never really been in his life, she sat up and listened, watch-ing his face the whole time. "I didn't know he mattered so much to you," she said when he had finished.

"Everyone's father matters," he said, turning away.

There were small miracles everywhere. Matt saw them, with his easy, optimistic outlook and his eye for the singularity of things.

The kids down the side street where he walked Mahalia to the park stuck a whole packet of incense sticks in two rows in the dirt outside their ramshackle wooden house and lit them. The cheap floral odor permeated the air, and the smoke drifted about in skinny lines from each stick, and Matt smiled to see the kids hobbling about in bare feet in their stony front yard, admiring the effect.

He saw a flock of sparrows on the rim of a garbage bin, jumping first one way and then another, a moving posse of birds, a circlet of brown feathered flowers.

And in the grounds of the Conservatorium where Eliza sang, he saw, from down the street, how two gigantic old fig trees rode the wind like a pair of galleons, their leaves an enormous ballooning sail against a darkened storm-cloud sky. Magpies tossed themselves in and out of the high branches, caroling to each other. Matt stopped to look. *Well, shit,* he said to himself, and he picked Mahalia up out of her stroller. "Look, Mahalia, can you see those trees? You'll go a long way before you see trees like that again."

Mahalia waved her arms at the sky. Her mouth was like an O.

"Gain," she said, "gain," like a maestro commanding a performance.

"No, Mahalia, you mightn't see a sight like that again," said Matt. Because he knew that you never always looked. The trees might be like that again, but he might never again notice them.

Mahalia was growing so fast that each day brought something new she could do, something he would never see again. He marked each day off in his mind, the date emblazoned in his heart, wanting to make the most of it, remembering how Emmy had said that it was a sin to let days pass unregarded. He allowed his mother to take photographs of Mahalia without protesting that she was fussing too much. He understood for the first time why people wanted to capture moments on film. However imperfectly the camera might record it, a snapshot was something, an aid to the memory. And he thought that one day Emmy might want to see them.

Mahalia had grown into such a *person* that it shocked Matt at times, the force of her will, her desire, her determination to do things. Mahalia was unstoppable; she was like a weight rolling downhill, gathering in momentum.

The day she took her first steps Matt realized there were moments so fleeting and so memorable that a photograph could never do them justice.

He was sitting in the front room downstairs, browsing through a magazine while Mahalia played. She had pulled herself up onto the barricade at the door, and amused herself by throwing things out onto the footpath. She threw her cup with the spout and lid. She threw one of her teddies, and she threw the board book her grandmother had given her. Then she started to cry, for she realized she wanted them back. Matt was about to haul himself up to fetch them for her when a woman walking past stopped and picked Mahalia's things up and gave them back to her, one by one. "There, is that what you want?" she said. Mahalia smiled, showing her teeth, and the tears that clung to her face looked superfluous now. She threw all her things onto the floor and waved to the woman as she continued down the street.

Matt saw her turn and catch sight of a laundry basket close by; he held his breath because he could tell what she was about to do. She let go of the barricade and walked a couple of steps (very wobbly and unsteady: her first steps!) to the basket, which was just the right height for her to grasp the top of once she got there. She chuckled to herself at her prowess. It was a private achievement; she hadn't noticed Matt watching her.

Then she found that by pushing herself forward, she could use the basket as a support and follow it along the floor. Matt watched, amazed, as Mahalia and the basket made their way across the floor. Then she caught his eye and laughed.

Matt went closer to her and crouched down immediately so that he was at her level. She let go of the basket and tottered, on unsteady legs, across the floor toward his outstretched hands. She made it into the safety of his arms without falling, and they both laughed and laughed as Matt rolled onto the floor with Mahalia clasped to his chest.

13

Eliza cut Mahalia's hair for her first birthday.

"I was always good with kids," she said. "They usually hate it—it's real hard to get them to sit still." She sat Mahalia in her high chair out in the backyard and snipped away at the soft dark curls.

"Thought you said you were never going to cut hair again," said Matt lazily, watching from the door of the kitchen.

"That's for a living. Friends are different." She gave Mahalia a small plastic mirror to hold. "Whatever you do, don't chuck it," she told her. After sucking on it for a while, Mahalia noticed that she could catch small glimpses of herself in it.

"Hold still—just a few more snips. There—now you look lovely. All those long straggly bits trimmed off. Now . . . look at yourself."

Eliza held a larger mirror up to Mahalia's face. "That's *you*, Mahalia!"

Matt would always remember her grave apprehension of herself for the first time.

Next morning Matt was woken by Mahalia standing in her crib rattling the bars and talking about the "hor." She pointed with her arm to somewhere that meant outside and yonder. The books that Matt put in her crib every night after she'd fallen asleep, hoping they'd amuse her in the morning, had already been looked at and thrown out onto the floor. "Hor," said Mahalia urgently. She saw that Matt was awake and that she almost had his attention.

Matt groaned. "Okay, Mahalia. We'll go and see the horse this morning." He threw back the sheet and got out of bed. "But first," he said, with his biggest smile, "happy birthday!"

Mahalia giggled when he lifted her from the crib and covered her in kisses. And she looked delighted and amused when Eliza sang her an elaborate "Happy Birthday" at breakfast and presented her with a parcel. She tasted the wrapping paper for a long time till Eliza showed her how to unwrap it. It was a book—an Aboriginal legend called *The Giant Devil Dingo*. When Mahalia saw the giant dingo on the cover, she pointed to it and said, "Hor."

"Oh, you, everything's a hor, isn't it?" said Matt. "That's a dog. A big dog."

Virginia sauntered her thin, leggy way into the kitchen. "Mahalia!" she said, and held out her arms wide. Mahalia looked up at her and smiled. "Happy birthday!"

Virginia plopped a parcel onto the tray of Mahalia's high chair. Mahalia was a fast learner; she knew now how to unwrap a parcel to find what was inside. It was a horse, made of solid molded plastic.

"Hor!" she said immediately. And then put the head straight into her mouth.

On the way to the horse paddock afterward, she urged the stroller to go faster with back-and-forth movements, pushing against the safety strap. "Hor! Hor!" she said, and pointed up the street. They came to the dogs. "Hor!" said Mahalia, pointing at Teg.

"That's a dog. That's Teg. And that's Tessa."

They walked on to the horses. Mahalia leaned forward in Matt's arms to smell them, wrinkling up her nose and showing her teeth with the pleasure of it.

"Do they stink, Mahalia?"

She looked around at him at the sound of her own name and pointed to the horse. "Hor," she said, as if she were revealing a remarkable fact to him.

On the far side of the paddock was a brown cow with a circle of white ibises standing all the way around it. The cow ate unconcernedly, but the ibises seemed to be worshiping the cow, paying homage to the cow.

"Maybe it's the cow's birthday, Mahalia, and they're wishing it happy birthday. Look. See the cow?"

Mahalia knew cows from the book Eliza read to her. "Moo!" she said.

They held a small birthday party. Just a cake, with Matt and his mother and Eliza and Virginia. Matt hadn't wanted a fuss. He wasn't in the mood for it, but his mother said they must have *something* and offered to make the cake.

Mahalia blew out her own candles, with help from Matt and a great deal of spitting. She leaned forward from Matt's arms and sucked the icing off the slice of cake that Matt's mother held out for her. "Hey, you lazy little bugga!" said Virginia. "Hang on to the cake yourself!"

Mahalia

They gave her a slice to hold and she squished it several times between her fingers before shoving the mush into her mouth, laughing with her mouth wide open.

Matt's mother and Eliza cleaned the kitchen together afterward. They got on remarkably well: had a matter-of-fact way of looking into each other's eyes, and didn't get under each other's feet.

Matt only overheard snatches of their conversation as he moved from the backyard, through the kitchen, and back again, attending to Mahalia:

". . . is just the best thing . . . ," said Eliza (she must be talking about singing).

". . . I'll never make a living from it . . ." (his mother's mask-making).

". . . Mahalia's his project now . . ." (they were talking about him!).

Kent arrived, and Eliza tossed her tea towel over the back of a chair. She crammed a bike helmet over her head, pulled on her boots and a jacket, and roared off on the back of his bike.

"She's beautiful, isn't she?" said his mother. "She's getting to that age. . . ."

"What age?" asked Matt.

His mother looked up, as though she had forgotten he was there. "Oh, when young women are really beautiful," she said vaguely. "What is she? Twenty-five?"

"Twenty-two," said Matt. It seemed that the whole world was older than him.

When she was almost ready to go home, his mother brought out a present from Emmy (Matt had sent her a letter with his address on it, but she always assumed he wouldn't be there long and sent everything to his mother).

"I didn't want to interrupt the party," she said.

Matt didn't know a present could be so painful. He thought of Emmy, how she had once gazed at Mahalia, and knew it had been painfully chosen. He put it aside for later.

"One year old," said Matt's mother wistfully as she prepared to leave. "It seems no time since you were that age. And now look at you. . . . You're doing so well with her, you know. She's a great kid." She put her arm round Matt's shoulder.

Matt looked at her in amazement. He thought he'd been struggling, always. The sleepless nights. Those times when he could kill for sleep. The times he just wanted to make her *shut up*. The struggle with money. The vulnerable, sometimes nebulous feeling he nearly always carried with him, that he was struggling to simply exist in the world.

And he'd needed so much help, in the end. He'd wanted to look after Mahalia on his own—to show he could do it. But he'd had help all along the way. From Charmian, and Eliza, and Virginia. Otis, even, in his way. And his mother, even his mother had helped, just by always being there, even though he'd refused most of her direct offers of help.

"Make sure you make the most of her, won't you?" she said. "They don't stay this age forever."

"I will," said Matt, surprised. "I do."

In the long months before Mahalia's birth, Emmy and Matt had lain together, limbs entwined, and talked of the mystery of it all.

Mahalia

They somehow envisaged their baby born under a tree some-where, a broad tree with a canopy of sheltering branches, a vast, maternal fig, perhaps, and the mystery and wonder of the world would bless them all.

The idea of the tree had been a dream, really, because they knew for a long time that their baby would be born in a hospital. Emmy had wanted a midwife but had been told she was too young, that a hospital would be safer. (And even a midwife would have drawn the line at a tree!)

Emmy had looked around at the gleaming labor room, a place of white sheets and stainless steel. There was a forest mural cover-ing one wall, a laughable attempt to make the place look natural.

"It's . . . so *ordinary*, really," said Emmy softly, looking around her.

"It *is* ordinary," said the nurse briskly. "Just a natural ordinary thing." She pulled a curtain across and bustled about with equipment.

Matt squeezed Emmy's hand and smiled. He'd known what she meant. It was far removed from their tree.

Matt watched as Emmy's concentration centered itself some-where in the middle of her being, so that he, and the nurses, and the labor ward weren't there at all. She had been like this often in the last few weeks: concentrated, thoughtful, far from him.

When she had pushed Mahalia into the world, Matt had been struck by how much *work* it had been. It required every bit of concentration she possessed. Her breath was heavy. A film of sweat slicked her face, and Matt wiped it away with a cool wash-cloth. It was all sheer effort and will, more work than toiling all day in the hot sun.

* * *

Matt was woken by Eliza coming home in the early hours of the morning; he listened as the motorbike idled in the street while she found the key to the door. Then the bike departed and Matt heard her Blundstones hitting the floor of the front room. He imagined her bare feet creeping up the stairs as she tried not to wake anyone. (Virginia, last week, said, "Do you have to sound like a baby elephant? Some people need their sleep, you know!")

There was a faint scent and a rustle of clothing as she passed his room, and the sound of her door closing.

Matt turned over in bed and listened to Mahalia's breathing, slow and even. She was one year old. He'd got her this far. It was an achievement, he supposed, but anxiety still gnawed at him. His doubts beat in his head like a drum. He got up abruptly and walked out onto the balcony, feeling sure that he wouldn't sleep tonight. The streetlights shone onto him, making an artificial twilight. He heard the faint voices of people walking up the street on their way home from somewhere, and the sounds of human life soothed him. Their laughter wrapped the night in comfort. The black dog, Voucher, trotted along the pavement opposite, looking purposeful, the way dogs do when they're on the move.

Suddenly he felt blessed that Mahalia was healthy, and alive, and with him. He went back to bed and pulled the sheet up over himself. Matt laughed aloud in the dark. A whole year! She'd been part of his life a whole year! He lay listening to Mahalia's merciful, light breathing. The house was so silent he thought he could hear the beat of her heart, the swoosh of blood through her veins, and the slow, certain growth of every cell in her body.

14

Matt's guitar appeared in the front room one day. BLUES IS THE MUSIC THAT HEALS said the case, white letters standing out in the gloom. The house was still cool; it had the tranquil, composed calm of a place remembering the night. Through the door the street shone in a bright square of light.

The guitar had been hidden from view of the street by a cardboard box. Matt saw it immediately as he came down the stairs in the morning. He put Mahalia down onto the floor, and she staggered away at once into the kitchen, where she could hear Virginia making breakfast. "Hey, Mahalia, *babeee!*" Virginia called. Mahalia ran to her, her arms waving in the air to steady herself, all the better to be scooped from the floor and into the air.

Matt rubbed the dull, textured surface of the guitar case. He hefted the weight and clicked open the catches, half-fearing that it would be filled with something else, that the weight would be something other than guitar. It wasn't. The white body of the guitar gleamed.

Matt smiled.

It was his birthday.

* * *

Otis was at home, in bed. "Don't get me up! It's the weekend."

Matt wrestled him off the bed and onto the floor. "You shouldn't have done it, man."

"Done what?" Otis stood up and wiped his eyes, which were filled with tears from laughing and trying not to. Matt hooked his foot round Otis's leg and brought him down again. Otis regained his feet at once. Matt grabbed him by the shoulders and head-butted him, and this time Otis fought back.

It was a satisfying tussle. Matt hadn't wrestled with Otis for a long time, not since Mahalia was born. He'd always had her strapped to his chest or clinging in his arms, but at this moment she was in the kitchen with Charmian.

"But," said Matt when they were both sitting back on the bed, panting with the exertion, "I'm paying you back for it as soon as I get some money."

"If you like," said Otis. He knew about pride. "But only some of it. It *is* ya birthday. I got sick of you playing Alan's old heap of shit. That guitar of his is crap," he said happily. "And you can try out for that band now. You want to, don't you?"

Matt pushed his hair away from his forehead and widened his eyes at the possibility. "Don't know," he said.

In the kitchen Mahalia was playing hide-and-seek with Charmian from underneath a towel, her face alive with delight every time Charmian "found" her.

"Hey, this baby had a birthday and you didn't ask me?" said Charmian, her face reproachful.

There were photos of Mahalia now, along with all the framed pictures of family and friends that covered the walls of the living room.

"It was just a little birthday," said Matt, embarrassed.

"Just a little cake," said Otis, grinning; he wasn't at all sad he hadn't been asked.

"Just a little birthday." Charmian was disgusted with him. "The first one! That's a big birthday! Only a little number but a big day!"

Charmian's family had had some bad luck. Her daughter's husband had got drunk and burned down the house they lived in (a big thing in a small city; it was in the local paper), so she and her kids were staying with Charmian and Alan and Otis until they could get another place. The house was overflowing with people, but houses were expandable, weren't they: there was always room for more. Charmian's normally placid face was weary. She'd come back after months in Kempsey with her relatives, and now this. But she'd met someone down there, and the thought of him brought a sly smile to her face.

"I'm tired," she said. "Think I'll go down south again, get me some lovin'."

Matt wished he could get some loving himself. He might have a guitar again, but he also was lonely, and filled with weariness.

He hitched to his mother's that afternoon, the evening of his birthday, hoping that the place would not close in on him like a Venus flytrap. He dreaded being drawn back into it. It would be easy. It would be like reclining onto a bed of moss and letting it grow over you. It would be like finding yourself in a part of the rainforest where the lawyer cane ("wait-a-while!") grows thick, its toothed vines catching hold of your clothing.

He was eighteen. Old enough to do lots of things. Old enough now to be a father.

His mother's house was filled with contradictions. It was in the middle of the forest, closed in, claustrophobic. And yet, perched as it was on the side of the mountain, there were places where you could look out and see over the whole forested valley, so that it was outward-looking and expansive. It was full of doors and windows, and yet, in places, there were no doors, just gaps where a door should be. He wanted to be independent, and yet his mother was always there.

His father had always been an unspoken presence. The fact of Matt's existence made him ever-present. As always, there was something from him for Matt's birthday. This year it was a check: a nice amount, two hundred dollars. Perhaps he thought Matt was too old now for other presents. Matt folded the check and put it beside him on the table. He could pay Otis back some of the money for the guitar.

He remembered other birthdays. The fun he and his mother had had.

"Hey," said Matt, smiling, "remember the year you gave me the bike for my birthday? And I persuaded you to have a go on it?"

She sat up and laughed at the memory.

"You hadn't ridden one for years," said Matt. "And you got on it and took off down the drive. . . ."

"It sort of took off with *me*," she said, "like some kind of animal with a mind of its own."

"And you yelled, 'Help, help,' but you had to keep pedaling to stay upright, and you went out onto the road and halfway down the hill before you found the brakes. We both laughed so hard I thought I was going to be sick," said Matt.

"You made me learn to ride it again properly after that," said his mother. "It kept me fit for a while."

"Matt," she said, as if out of the blue, but it was obvious she'd been thinking about it for some time, "why don't you let me teach you to drive? You're eighteen now. You could've had your license for a year."

Matt scratched the back of his neck and shook his head. "I'll never get a car."

"If you could drive you could borrow mine."

Matt sighed and shook his head. "Yeah, I know. But I don't know that I want to get around that way."

"Most young men can't wait to get their license."

"I'm not most young men."

"Why are you so stubborn? And anyway, you *might* get a car one day." His mother started to collect the plates. "Think about it," she said, not wanting to quarrel on his birthday. "The longer you put it off, the harder it'll get."

Mahalia had been sitting in her high chair, watching them and laughing because they were laughing. But when the conversation took a serious turn, she'd started to fuss. Matt pushed back his chair. "Come on," he said to her, "I'll take you for a walk outside." She put her arms around his neck and he lifted her onto his hip.

In the garden, she walked along beside him, holding his hand, her bare feet curling up on the rough ground, her toes like pale grubs. He lifted her up and tossed her into the air and caught her. Mahalia loved that. He took hold of her feet and suspended her upside down. Spatial development. She held on tight and swung like a monkey, and he carried her, still upside down, her body clasped securely to his chest, to the gap in the trees where they could look out over the valley. It was all space, and distance; only an occasional cleared patch and a dull roof showed where there might be other people.

Matt turned Mahalia the right way up again and plopped her down onto the ground. When Mahalia saw her grandmother come out to join them, she waved her arms and staggered across the grass toward her.

"Gosh, you're a little grub," said his mother. "You've got lunch all over you. Do you feel like a bath?"

"Ba," said Mahalia, gesturing toward the house.

Matt's mother ran some water into the big bathtub and Mahalia was so keen to get in, she helped her grandmother remove her clothes by lifting her arms and legs at the right moments. Matt's mother knelt beside the bath and steadied Mahalia's slippery body in the water.

Matt came inside and leaned in the bathroom doorway and watched, a rueful smile on his face. Once, he'd said to his mother, "I'll bathe her. She's my baby, okay?" As if his mother, by merely doing something for Mahalia, could alter the fact that she was. There was such a thing, he thought, as being too independent. And he was eighteen now.

"Thanks for the offer to teach me to drive," said Matt, surprising himself. "I think I'll take you up on it. I'll go to the RTA and get the learner's book, yeah?"

Mahalia had her first visit to Emmy's mother on her own, for a whole day. She left cheerfully, strapped into the car seat, waving to Matt through the side window as the car pulled away. He felt her absence. His arms were empty. He was used to hefting the weight of her, taking her everywhere. He was childless for the first time in over a year.

Virginia and Eliza had gone out already. He lay on his bed and listened to the silence in the house. He picked up BLUES IS THE MUSIC THAT HEALS and strummed a few disconsolate notes, and the sound only made him sadder. It would have filled up his day if he could've jammed with Otis, but he'd be at school. For a moment Matt thought of school with something close to nostalgia: there were always people there to talk to, at least. He wished Eliza were in the house, singing—when she belted out a song it wasn't a lonesome sound. It filled up the world with expectation.

"Arr, shit!"

Matt hauled himself up off the bed and set about tidying the room. He took in yesterday's clothes and diapers from the line on the veranda and folded them. The sheets hadn't been washed for ages, so he stripped his bed and the crib and shoved it all into a garbage bag to take down to the Laundromat.

In the street he saw the dogs, Teg and Tessa. "Hi, Teg! Hi, Tessa!" he said in the high voice he used when saying something for Mahalia's benefit. He stopped, feeling stupid. They wagged their tails at him anyway and panted, their blue tongues hanging out.

He found himself, in the slow, hot, childless afternoon, bumping into Elijah, who was just about to knock on his front door. He'd got the address from Matt's mother. Elijah was back from fruit picking, and he had a dog, a fierce-looking dingo-ridgeback cross. "This is Jess," said Elijah, "and it depends who you are, how she likes ya."

Jess wagged her tail at Matt.

Matt was pleased to see Elijah, who looked at him speculatively. "You've had ya hair cut, mate!" he said, nodding cynically. Elijah's hair was also shorter. He looked older and more muscular, and his eyes had a defensive, challenging look.

They wandered down Matt's street to where paddocks led to their old school, and they sat on the edge of the football field, sharing a durry that Elijah took from a back pocket.

"Remember sneaking off from there?" said Elijah, nodding toward the timber, high-set buildings of the school. "Best thing we ever did."

"Did you go fruit picking?" said Matt. "Make any money?"

"Went all the way to Shep," said Elijah, "Shepparton. In Victoria. Got a job as a farm laborer for a while. They work ya, those blokes, I tell ya, ten, thirteen hours a day, eight days without a break. Got to the eighth day I collapsed in the heat." He laughed bitterly. His mouth turned down. "There was this guy, a *pen-pusher* from Bondi, started working there. Did three days and collapsed. This bastard of an owner says to him, 'I downed you after three days. Took me eight to down Elijah.'"

He took a sour kind of pride in this. "And then, when they don't want ya, when the weather's bad, it's back to Centrelink. Those bastards know not to muck me and Jess around now. After the few go-ins I had with 'em. They see me comin' with Jess and they're all politeness. I say to Jess, 'We're goin' down to Centrelink. . . .'"

When she heard the word *Centrelink,* Jess turned her orange head and growled.

"That's right, isn't it, Jess? *Centrelink!*"

Jess growled again.

"Jess is the *scourge* of Centrelink. This woman says to me, 'I'd appreciate it if you left your dog outside. We don't permit animals in here.'"

"'Listen,' I said. 'This dog goes where I go.' You've got to call the buggers' bluff. They're happy if you don't want a job. But when you *want* a job, when you *demand* a job, when you want to know why the bastards who'll employ you on a day-to-day basis, like, won't give you any *permanent* employment, when they hire and fire you just like that. . . . Anyway, me and Jess are *real* well known at Shepparton Centrelink."

Elijah laughed again. He was older, harder.

"Did you make any money?" said Matt.

"Made it, and spent it." He sighed. "Made just about enough to keep me and Jess alive. Still got your baby?"

Matt nodded. "She's visiting Emmy's parents today."

Elijah nodded and pulled a face. He had an almost constant downward turn to his mouth now. "You could get them to look after her all the time, probably," he said.

"But I don't want them to," said Matt, amazed that Elijah could suggest such a thing. "She's mine."

The truth was that when Matt was without Mahalia, he felt that something was missing. It was an uneasy feeling, a sense that he'd left something behind, that there was something he should have remembered that he'd forgotten. It was too easy to walk down the street without a baby in tow. No getting together all the stuff you had to take, no unfolding the stroller or folding it up again, maneuvering it through doors and over curbs, no talking con-

stantly, soothing and reassuring. You just stood up and you . . .
went. It was unnatural.

With Mahalia still not due back till later in the afternoon,
Matt, in his aimlessness, ended up at the Conservatorium,
waiting for Eliza. He sat under a fig tree, watching people come
and go.

SUBVERT THE DOMINANT PARADIGM said the graffiti on the wall.

This annoyed Matt because he didn't even know how to pro-
nounce PARADIGM, let alone what it meant. Maybe he should go
back to school (go to TAFE, like Virginia!), learn some big words,
make something of himself.

At last Eliza emerged, wheeling her bicycle down the steps
because she had no bike lock and always took it inside for safe-
keeping. Kent was with her. They saw Matt and came over to him.

"What's that mean?" Matt said, indicating the graffiti with a
movement of his head.

"Why so many poor?" said Eliza. "Good question, when the
country's meant to be so prosperous."

"You mean 'paradigm'?" said Kent, knowing at once what
Matt was getting at. He said it so it rhymed with "dime." "It
means a way of looking at things. The concept that dominates
this society." His dark bright eyes looked keenly at Matt.

"Which is?" Matt wondered why people had to use such difficult words.

Kent grinned. "How about: *Work. Consume. Die?* No, but
really, you tell me what it is."

"Something like that," Matt grunted.

"It comes from a Greek word meaning a pattern."

"You just know that?"

"Nah, had to look it up in a dictionary when I saw that graffiti." Kent grinned at him.

Matt laughed. "It could be *paradiddle*. Subvert the dominant paradiddle. You know, that hand pattern for drumming . . . right, left, right right, left left—"

"Or right, right, right, right . . . maybe that's the dominant paradiddle?" interrupted Kent, laughing.

"Oh, what are you *on*?" said Eliza, impatient with the conversation. She got onto her bike. "I'll leave you blokes to it!" she yelled, her head turned to one side so they'd hear her as she rode off.

"Hey," said Kent. "A little bird told me that you had your bass back. How about coming for a jam with us? See how you go. We're meeting on Saturday afternoon, shed in the back of my place. Eliza'll give you the address."

The shed backed onto a laneway and they left the roller door open to let in light and air. Matt brought his guitar, and Mahalia, and toys to keep her amused, and food, and a bag of diapers and spare clothes. He was used to packing up all that stuff now.

He was worried that she'd go out onto the street, so they improvised a barricade from an old ladder. It was something of a deterrent to Mahalia, but she would still be able to climb over it, and Matt had to constantly turn around to check out where she was.

Matt wanted to play well today. He wanted to get into the band. He knew a lot of guitarists played bass from necessity because their band needed a bass player, but they really preferred to be on guitar. But Matt actually liked being part of the rhythm rather than the melody. He found great delight in providing the background notes.

Besides Matt on bass and Kent on guitar, there was another guitarist, Brian, who was very short and muscular and beautiful, with long black curly hair and a beatific smile almost always on his face. The drummer was Pete, a tall thin man with an unshaven face and multiple piercings in his ears and nose. There was also a trumpet player, whose name Matt didn't catch, for he arrived when Mahalia had started up a slow persistent whine, holding her arms up for Matt to lift her, and then shaking her head and wanting to get down again, so that Matt missed most of Kent's introduction.

Matt settled Mahalia with a toy car to look at and a bottle full of water with a nipple to suck on. Though she mostly drank from a cup, he still used a bottle to comfort her, and now he laid her down on a beanbag in the corner. She held the bottle with one hand and the car in the other, and her eyes followed his every move. She was wary of this new place, dark and dank and full of new people.

"You know that Dan Penn song 'Cry Like a Man'?" Kent asked him.

Matt shook his head. "Play it and I'll pick it up."

They started to play, straggling into the song, and tentative at first, but Matt soon picked up the rhythm. ". . . and cry, cry, cry like a man," it went.

Mahalia couldn't make it to the end of the song without starting to cry herself. She sat up and held the nipple of the bottle in her mouth and wailed, her face damp and flushed. Matt dashed over to her, his guitar dangling round his neck, steadying it with one hand while he picked Mahalia up with the other. "Look, sorry," he said to the others over his shoulder. "I won't be a sec. . . ."

An old man appeared at the door of the shed, dressed in work pants held up by a rope. He was longhaired and gray-bearded. "Brian!" he yelled, his face bright with happiness.

Brian's face lit up. "Andreas! Come in!"

The old man stepped heavily over the makeshift barricade. "I heard you play!" he bellowed. "Can I stay and watch?"

Brian nodded and introduced him to Matt. "Matt, this is Andreas."

Matt smiled vaguely, distracted by Mahalia.

"Guess where I am from!" Andreas demanded of Matt, not noticing how flustered he was. Matt shrugged. Andreas spoke each word distinctly, in an accent he couldn't identify.

"*Alaska!*" Andreas yelled in an exaggerated American accent. "But I was born in Austria."

Mahalia had finished her water and still wanted more to drink. Matt seized a large bottle of chocolate milk that Kent had put on top of the amp and poured some into her bottle.

"I came to Australia forty years ago. Saw it in *National Geographic*. Came out on a boat. Guess which port I arrived at!"

"Brisbane?" hazarded Matt.

"No! *Fremantle!*" Nothing Andreas said was in anything less than a shout. The others in the band tuned their instruments, ignoring him. Mahalia was startled by all the yelling and started to cry.

"I'm divorced from my wife, but we still talk! Guess why!"

Matt shrugged. He rubbed Mahalia's back, trying to soothe her.

"We have thirteen grandchildren!"

"Hey, Andreas," said Brian gently. "We need to start and you're disturbing the baby. Shhh!" he put his fingers to his lips with a smile, and Andreas was obediently silent. He went over to a chair and sat quietly, preparing to watch them.

Matt laid Mahalia back on the beanbag, where she sucked on the bottle of chocolate milk.

"Let's go," said Kent. " 'Cry Like a Man.' "

They got almost to the end of the song before Mahalia started up again. She sat up and held the nipple of the bottle between her teeth again and she cried, red-faced and angry. Leaning forward, she bit suddenly and fiercely at the nipple, and bit it right off. The bottle fell to the floor and the milk spilled out. Just as Matt arrived to mop it all up, she got to her feet, tottered forward, and vomited into Brian's open guitar case.

By that night Mahalia had a full-blown fever. She cried and tossed and fretted. It was a hot night anyway, a night to sleep with a sheet only, and Matt dampened some washcloths with cold water and put them to her forehead. It helped for a while, but then she vomited again, and contined to vomit throughout the night. Matt was exhausted with getting up and down to her. All his sheets and towels were soon soaking in the bathtub.

Eliza and Virginia got up and looked on at his struggles with her, helpless. Finally, long after she had anything left to vomit up, Mahalia was on her knees in her crib, retching. She was pale and weak, and Matt looked up at Eliza, who sat at the end of his bed, and said, "I'm going to take her to the hospital. What do you think?"

Eliza nodded.

He'd needed someone to consult. It was hard making a

decision on your own. Eliza went out to a phone box to call a taxi and went to the hospital with him.

The doctor was the same one who'd attended to his cut hand. Matt felt a vague sense of shame, as if he were a person who couldn't manage his life, who turned up uselessly at hospitals at odd hours. The lights shone, white and intrusive, and Mahalia squinted into the glare. Her hair was damp. She was crumpled with exhaustion. Usually robust and plump, she looked a tiny scrap in just singlet and diaper.

"Is she still breast-fed?" said the doctor to Eliza.

"Um—no," said Eliza. "She's weaned," loyally not dispelling the assumption that she was Mahalia's mother.

"Well, it's not serious," said the doctor, "if you don't let her get dehydrated. She has gastroenteritis—most babies seem to get it at about this stage. But you need to keep the fluids up to her." He wrote down the name of some stuff they could use. "I'll give her something now and something you can take home and give her until you can get to a drugstore."

They went back in a taxi, Mahalia asleep at last in Matt's arms. "The thing is," said Matt, "you just don't *know*, and in the middle of the night, when she looks like that. . . ." He hated to be seen as an incompetent parent, but he was relieved that she'd be all right.

"You did the right thing," said Eliza, and patted his arm as she peered out at the night from the back of the taxi. "You weren't to know what it was."

When they got home, Matt put Mahalia to bed and kissed her lightly on her damp, sick-smelling little head. Afterward, he and

Eliza sat for a while together at the kitchen table, drinking tea in an exhausted companionship.

When Matt finally got to bed, the sky had started to become pale. He listened to Mahalia's light even breathing, the blessed silence of her sleep, and he hugged his arms around himself. He thought, as he often did before sleep, of Emmy, but this time he had trouble remembering her face.

She'd worn a red dress the day she left, and carried the rest of her clothes in a small black bag. She'd looked at him with a face full of distress. "Look, I have to get away for a while. You'll be all right with the baby . . . ?" She'd fled on a bus, not looking back at them.

At first, when she'd gone, he'd remembered only her mouth; her mouth and her smile and her fine white teeth. But then what he missed was the sheer fact that she wasn't there with them; he had no one to consult, no one to sleep beside at night.

Now he remembered the red dress, a short red dress with a ruffle round the neck. And now it hit him that he'd been a fool for months. It was over between them, and she wasn't coming back, wasn't coming back.

And he knew that if she did, it wouldn't be for him.

15

A week later, on an ordinary day, when she stood at the front door, her face, which Matt thought he'd forgotten, was alive to him again. Her eyes, almond-shaped, brown, deep-set in her face, were just as he remembered. So were the freckles scattered across her nose. Her mass of thick soft brown hair, pushed back behind her ears, was exactly the same. It had seemed an eternity since he'd seen her, but now, with her there so suddenly, no time seemed to have passed at all.

Emmy licked her lips in a way that was utterly characteristic of her, her tongue pausing on the lower lip. Then she smiled, uncertainly at first, then with her whole face. "Hello," she said. "You're at home." She looked embarrassed, perhaps at saying such a dumb, obvious thing.

"I'm sorry to surprise you," she went on quickly. "But I didn't know what else to do. I got home yesterday, and I couldn't wait. You don't have a phone. . . ."

She stepped forward and put her arms around him. He caught the familiar scent of her hair; it was warm from the sun, and smelled of moist brown leaves. She gave an embarrassed laugh. "I don't know what to say. Can I see Mahalia?"

144

He took her through to the backyard, gesturing for her to go ahead of him. He'd forgotten how small she was, yet how rounded and curved. She wore a tight-fitting top, and a short skirt that showed the shape of her hips. Halfway down the hall to the kitchen she turned and glanced up at him frankly without pausing in her brisk stride.

Mahalia was busy with a bucket and spade in a sandpit he'd made in the corner. "Da?" she said as he arrived. She turned to greet him, waved the spade in the air, lost her balance, and landed on her bottom. Saving face, she scrambled to her feet immediately and smiled at them both.

Emmy crouched down to look at her better. So did Matt. Mahalia came over to him, unsteady still on her legs, and handed him one of her toy cars. His arms went round her, and she snuggled shyly against his shoulder and peeped out at Emmy from her safe vantage point. Something about their demeanor alerted her that this was no ordinary stranger.

"You got back yesterday?" he asked. "You're staying with your mother?"

"Yes."

He was thankful that Eliza and Virginia were out. He made a cup of tea, and Emmy came into the kitchen to drink it, looking out through the back door at Mahalia, who played in her sandpit and talked to herself, exclaiming and making sounds of wonder.

Emmy sat and stared out into the yard. He couldn't see her face. Then he saw that she was crying silently to herself, and he went over to her and put his arms around her.

But she pushed him gently away. Embarrassed, he went to the sink and started to clatter dirty plates. Tears came to his eyes and he blinked them away. He would not, would not, he thought, allow memories of their life together to intrude now.

Eliza arrived home, clattering her bike through the front door and calling out a cheerful greeting to whoever might be in the house. She appeared for a moment at the kitchen door, and went away just as quickly without saying a word.

"Do you want to take her up to the park?" said Matt, and Emmy nodded. Once there, they sat, cross-legged, facing each other on the grass.

Matt thought that they might be able to talk, but Mahalia called out urgently from the swing, where she stood holding on to the seat, unable to get on. It wasn't a word, just a sound, but the meaning was clear. She wanted to be pushed.

So Matt pushed her, and Emmy stood by and watched shyly. "She's grown a lot," said Emmy, in a subdued, sad, husky voice. "In just seven months."

Emmy visited them again the next day.

She was happy to sit and watch Mahalia. She didn't rush her, or scare her by trying to pick her up too soon. She merely sat with a sad smile on her face and allowed Mahalia to play around her. Soon Mahalia came up to her and handed her a toy car: Mahalia was very keen on cars—she called them *broooms*.

Emmy reached out at last and touched her hair. Mahalia immediately put her hand to her head and glared at Emmy, pushing the hand away and rubbing her head as if someone had violated her. Then she smiled and lunged forward to grab Emmy by the leg. Emmy scooped her up at once and placed her on her lap. Mahalia squealed and tried to wriggle free, but by this time her shyness was a game, and she ended up lying back in Emmy's arms and gazing into her face, as if she recognized her.

Matt left them alone together. It occurred to him he could one-up Emmy by asserting his connection to Mahalia: by saying, "Come on, Mahalia, time for a bath," by hanging around and showing *he* was the one with the familiarity and authority, but he couldn't. When he saw Emmy gaze at her baby with such fear and longing, he knew he had no right to that.

"Do you want to give her a bath?" he said.

He ran some water into the bathtub and Mahalia was cooperative when Emmy undressed her. She loved a bath because she loved to experiment with water, and once in the tub, she filled the sponge with water and held it out in front of her and squeezed the water out again.

She kicked her legs back and forth in the water with excitement, letting it splash up over her chest and face. And then she conducted the whole experiment again, serious while she allowed the water to be absorbed into the sponge, excited when she was able to squeeze it out.

Matt wondered if Emmy would want to take Mahalia back. He thought of all his recent difficulties: the mess she'd made of his tryout with the band, the visit to the hospital. Life would be full of many more days like that. Treacherously, he allowed himself to imagine a life of freedom without the burden of a baby.

To restore the familiarity of his life he went the next afternoon to see Otis for the first time in ages. Otis was frowning over his books, "taking Year 12 too seriously," as Alan said from the doorway of his room. Mahalia went to look for Charmian and returned looking lost. "Not there, mate?" said Otis. "That's because she still down at Kempsey—don't know when she'll be back," and Mahalia seemed to understand him. He went and found some toys for her, and she sat on the floor between them, playing.

Because Matt was there, Otis's fingers reached out for his guitar, and he sat playing chords while Matt listened silently. Otis was still looking fit and sharp. "Do any good," said Matt, "with that girl you were interested in?" and Otis laughed, shamefaced. "What girl?" he said, and then, "Nah, no good. Forgotten about her already."

"Emmy came back," said Matt. "She's staying with her mother."

Otis took this in silently, and Matt was pleased he didn't ask more, had known he wouldn't; that was why he'd been able to mention it.

"Try out for that band?" Now it was Otis's turn to be nosy. Matt told him about Mahalia's spectacular vomit and Otis chuckled.

"The guys were okay about it," said Matt. "Pretended it didn't matter. I left straight after. Still feel bad."

"Good case?"

"Old Gibson Les Paul."

Otis winced.

"Dark red crushed-velvet lining."

"Man, man . . ."

Matt felt happier after seeing Otis, and afterward went to wait for Eliza at the Conservatorium. Whiling away the time, deliberately not thinking of Emmy, he sat out under the big camphor-laurel tree and watched people come and go. A short sturdy girl in a striped top and beret paced back and forth and talked into a mobile phone. A man in a Hawaiian shirt unlocked his bicycle, got onto it, and wobbled off, adjusting his sunglasses. A three-legged dog hopped along after its dreadlocked owners, with that hopeful expectant look that dogs have. It was a well-dressed dog, wearing a bandanna rakishly around its neck; the triangle of the scarf hung down and concealed the scar where the missing leg should be. Its owners had bought fish and chips for tea. "D'you want to eat down by the river?"

"Yes, let's!" They got into their van with their dog and drove off.

Matt watched them go. Everyone was purposeful and knew what they were doing except him.

"Dog!" said Mahalia urgently, pointing after the departing van.

"Yes, that's a dog," he said automatically.

Mahalia considered for a while and then she had another thought. "Horse!" she exclaimed, and pointed into the distance.

"Yep, we'll go and see the horse another day. Maybe tomorrow, eh? They're still your favorite animal, aren't they? Your mum likes horses." From now on, he realized, whatever was decided, Emmy would be a fact of their life. He saw no point in not mentioning her.

He strapped Mahalia back into her stroller. If Eliza didn't come out soon, he'd leave and make his way home by himself.

But then she came down the steps, wheeling her bicycle rapidly with a sort of *whooshing* motion that threatened to run away with her when she reached the bottom. She steadied herself and saw Matt standing there. Smiling, and without a word, she fell into step with him, wheeling her bike along the footpath beside Mahalia's stroller.

They passed a young guy only a bit older than Matt. Like Matt, he was thin, dressed in thin, poor, thrift-shop clothes. He wheeled an old bicycle with a toddler in a bike seat on the back. The child wore a helmet, and peered out from it like a little soldier. The father bumped the bicycle deliberately up and down as he walked. "Is that bouncy?" he asked.

"Yes!" said the child happily.

"I thought it might be!"

"I could get a kid's seat and helmet for Mahalia," said Eliza. "Then she could come riding with me. Should be able to pick something up at a garage sale."

"Yeah!" said Matt. Then he had another thought. "Or I could bring my old bike in from my mum's place, put a kid's seat on that. I've been meaning to for ages. That'd get us around a bit easier, instead of the stroller." He still hadn't been to try for his learner's permit.

They went home across the rattly metal walkway on the bridge and looked down at the slow weedy water. Matt cooked dinner and they ate it sitting on the edge of Eliza's herb garden. They left some for Virginia, who would probably come home late, starving hungry, and rave on in her jittery way while spooning food straight from the pot.

"Hey, come for a walk, I'll show you something," said Eliza, jumping up and holding her hand out to pull Matt to his feet. He carried Mahalia on his hip and they went down the lane till they came to the house with the permaculture garden, the place that

Matt liked to think of as the Garden of Eden. Eliza walked up the side and beckoned him to follow. The ground was damp from rain that morning.

"I noticed this the other day. The rose apples are ripe." Eliza led him to a spreading tree with an umbrella-like canopy. She reached up and plucked a yellow fruit about the size of a small plum and tore it in half. "Taste this." Matt tasted, and his taste buds recoiled. It was like eating perfume.

"It's like Turkish delight," said Eliza. "That rosewater taste. That's why it's called a rose apple." She offered some to Mahalia, but Mahalia turned her head away and wouldn't try it.

Eliza took Mahalia from Matt and held her, singing, softly at first, and then louder, improvising a song around Mahalia's name, looking into the baby's eyes and swinging her on her hip. Mahalia started to sing too, a soft tuneless sound, *la la la*.

Matt glanced up at the wooden house that towered above them on stilts. Eliza had lived here once, and had been sad here, yet she could still come back and enjoy the place.

"You said you were in love here," said Matt. "How did it go wrong?"

Eliza reached for another rose apple. "I'm not exactly sure. You get together with someone and it's wonderful at first and then it's just little things, isn't it? You find you're not so compatible anymore. At least, that's the way it was with me. I was so *in love* at the start that when the end came I felt that I'd been hit by a truck."

16

With Emmy back, but nothing resolved, Matt tried to get on with his everyday life, scrappy and aimless as it was. He didn't like to let Mahalia out of his sight now, but he let Virginia take her out shopping with her, as she used to do. Why should things be different now?

But after they'd been gone from the house only a little while, Matt longed to see Mahalia so much that he went out to see if he could find them. He hunted for them in the supermarket, peering down every aisle, his stomach a knot of irrational anxiety. He caught sight of Virginia's lanky body ambling along behind a trolley, her cap pushed up to the top of her head. Alarmed because he couldn't see Mahalia in the cart, he loped up the aisle, dodging shoppers, till with relief he saw her. She was pushing the trolley, singing a tuneless song as she went, and it went this way and that, bumping into people, steadied occasionally by Virginia, who grinned and apologized to the people they'd bumped into.

Virginia halted when she saw Matt and her face registered an instant realization of why he was there.

"Hey," said Matt. "Fancy running into you two." He picked Mahalia up and hefted the pleasing weight of her in his arms.

"Yeah," said Virginia, grinning at him generously, allowing him to save face. "Had to come in for something, did you?"

It seemed he was always losing her. Emmy took Mahalia to stay with her and her mother for the day. She came in her mother's car. "You can drive?" said Matt.

Emmy smiled at him with that old smile, happy with herself. "Charlotte taught me," she said. When he looked uncomprehending, she added, "My godmother? When I stayed with her?" Then she laughed and strapped Mahalia into the baby seat in the back, and with a smile and a wave and a backward glance at him, she ducked behind the wheel, started the engine, and drove off.

With Mahalia gone, Matt disgusted himself by getting drunk. He met Elijah, who had a fortuitous bottle of Bundy rum swinging from his fingers and his dog, Jess, following faithfully at his heels. They drank way too much, down by the river, and when Emmy delivered Mahalia back late in the afternoon, he hoped she couldn't smell his breath. He spewed it all up sometime in the middle of the night. "Mate, just look at you," said Virginia, shaking her head in the doorway of the bathroom. She helped clean him up and put him back to bed.

A few days later Emmy took Mahalia to stay the night with her. It would be the first night they'd spent away from each other. Matt felt Emmy was a stranger as she waited in his room while he packed up some of Mahalia's things. She still hadn't talked to him about what she wanted to do.

Emmy went out with Mahalia on her hip and a bag filled with her clothes. He listened desolately to her footsteps sounding all the way down the stairs and then, impulsively, ran after them and caught them up. Emmy looked up at him inquiringly.

"You'd better take her sun hat," he said, pulling it down from a cluster of hats near the door.

Emmy took it and her eyes met his briefly and frankly. "Look, Matt, I should tell you something. I'd like Mahalia to come and live with me."

His face must have registered his dismay. She hesitated, and said, "Think about it, yeah?"

The front door closed behind them.

Emmy's words beat a rhythm in his head. He went over and over them until they ceased to have any meaning. He paced the streets, seeing nothing. He didn't bother eating that day.

To distract himself he went out that night to a pub where Eliza was singing with a band. He didn't drink. He was stone-cold sober in a surge of people tipping back beer and spirits. The smell of alcohol nearly made him sick again.

"Don't worry about the other day," said Kent, appearing in the crowd and slapping Matt on the shoulder. "And Brian, he's cool—said he was about to replace the old lining in that case anyway. We're rehearsing again next week, so come round. Maybe you could get a baby-sitter?" Matt nodded, but playing in a band was the last thing on his mind.

Eliza's face was different on the darkened stage. Her face always had that look of intimacy when she sang, that *lostness* to the world that Otis had when he played the guitar, but tonight it seemed to Matt to be especially for him. He stood still and gazed at her from the edge of the room. Seeming to sense him, she swung around and looked him straight in the eyes for a moment, smiling. Then she turned away again, back to the room, and closed her eyes for a long time, listening only to the sound of her own voice.

Matt pushed his way outside, where his sober head reeled under the stars and the familiar summer air breathed upon his face like a faithful dog.

He went home; the house was silent. The backyard was lit only by the light shining out from the kitchen. Matt crouched in the sandpit and ran Mahalia's little cars around and around. He huddled into himself, made himself into a squatting, unthinking, hurting ball.

He'd sat there a long time, dazed and sad, when footsteps sounded in the kitchen.

"Matt? You home?"

"Yeah." He stood up. Eliza was in the doorway, stark against the light from inside the house.

"All alone in the dark?" she said.

It was a long time until Matt spoke. He didn't trust his voice.

"Emmy wants Mahalia," he said.

She understood at once. "What are you going to do?" She went to put an arm round his shoulder, but he pushed away from her.

He went to his room, full of desperate energy, and took all of Mahalia's clothes, jumbled as they were on the floor and in washing baskets, and folded them into a pile in a corner of the room. He stacked up her books and toys next to them, and stripped her crib of sheets.

He had no idea why he was doing this. He was packing her up. Tidying her away. Imagining the place without her. The wind chimes on the veranda rattled without pause. The sound sent an itch of irritation right through him, and he marched out and reefed them down and tossed them aside.

He went to Mahalia's tidied-away things and crouched in front of them, reaching out suddenly with desperate hands and scattering them everywhere.

All this he did in complete silence. He could hear only his own breath, panting softly.

He thought of living without her and a wave of pain passed up through his body in a ripple. He wanted to run somewhere to stop himself thinking, but had no idea where he could go.

So he switched off the light and lay in the dark, his breath coming in quick, deep gasps. He listened to the sound of his own breath as if it belonged to someone else. He heard Eliza come up the stairs and go to the bathroom. The door of her room closed quietly.

Matt curled into a ball with his face in the pillow. His eyes flooded with hot tears, and there came a strange, high sound, a kind of squeak, that he knew was coming from himself. He listened to it as if it had nothing to do with him at all. The sound changed to a sob; he felt his whole body was an instrument for the sound and the pain that played through him. He swallowed it all inside himself until he could bear it no longer.

He found himself standing in his dark room; the lights from the street threw moving shadows across it.

And then he was at Eliza's door. It had not been properly closed and he pushed it gently open. The room was moonlit and silent.

But she was not asleep. She sat up in bed and said, "Matt, what's wrong?"

He stood there, his eyes squeezed shut. He was still making sounds that seemed not to belong to him.

Eliza threw back the sheet. "Oh, Matt . . ."

He felt her hands grip his elbows from behind and lead him to the bed, where she sat him down on the edge. She didn't put on the light, but moved swiftly to her bedside table, where she lit a squat yellow candle. He could smell melting wax, and the room was suffused with a warm glow, as if she had lit a tiny sun. He was aware that the noise he'd been making had stopped.

Though it was a warm night, he was shivering. He saw Eliza's concerned face and the white satin of her nightdress as she plucked a red-and-black-checked blanket from an armchair and wrapped it around his shoulders. He huddled into it. She knelt in front of him. In the light from the candle he imagined for a moment that it was a lion kneeling there. He reached out to touch her face, expecting fur.

Her face was full of compassion, but not pity. "What are you feeling?" she said.

He didn't reply, but she persisted. "Tell me how you feel." The words were as steady and reliable as the tick of a clock.

Matt heard himself take a deep shuddering breath.

"Pain. Real, physical pain . . ."

She kept staring into his face.

"Like a wave, a current, running through my body . . . What will I do without her?" he said.

But she said nothing, simply continued to listen.

"I never allowed myself to ever think about the possibility of this. With my stupid optimism . . ." He felt the heat of tears beneath his eyelids again.

She reached out a hand and touched his face. "No crying," she said. "What else?"

"I feel that something has burst inside me. I've held it all in and not let on. It's been such a strain, not allowing myself to think too much, just getting on with looking after . . . her." He found he couldn't even say his baby's name. "Not knowing what was going to happen, but hoping . . ."

Eliza didn't prompt him, but looked steadily at him.

"Oh, not that Emmy would come back for *me*. Or maybe I did. I don't know what I hoped. I keep going over and over it but *nothing makes sense!*" The room blurred.

"Okay," he heard Eliza say. "You can cry now. I can see that I'm not going to be able to stop you."

Matt laughed and wiped his eyes and looked up at her. There was a tender expression on her face.

"Anyway," he said. "I like *you*." He reached out and his hand bumped into her face as if he were a sleepwalker. It connected with her nose, her mouth . . .

She bit his fingers gently. "Look, get into my bed and get some sleep. You know, just to be with someone."

17

In the morning Matt rose before Eliza was awake. She slept on her stomach, her arms flung above her head. He remembered having held her briefly during the night, but he awoke on the opposite side of the bed.

After hardly eating the day before, he was starving now; he piled cheese onto bread and ate it standing at the kitchen sink. Then he let himself out. All day he walked the streets, just walking, trying to keep his head empty. He rested for a while, lying on a bench in a park, covering his eyes with his arm to shield them from the sun.

In the afternoon he went back, for that was when Emmy was to drop Mahalia off. "Think about what I said," she said to him. "I'd like to talk about it soon." Then she was gone again.

They were the only ones home. Matt sat Mahalia on his bed and looked around the room. Her things were still scattered over the floor. Slowly, methodically, he packed them up.

"How about we go away for a holiday?" he said to her, squatting down and looking into her eyes. She gazed right back at him, right into his eyes, the way she had ever since she'd been born.

"Da!" she said happily, waving one fat arm in the air.

Mahalia

"Away!" he said, and stuffed things into a duffel bag. He went to the kitchen and took a few dried staples, potatoes, and pasta. After a moment's hesitation he wrote a note for Eliza. *Gone away for a few days.*

And he hefted Mahalia onto his hip and went out to the road, and before too long had managed to hitch out of town.

Matt took Mahalia to the place where he and Emmy had lived in the months before her birth, and for a week afterward. It was a camper perched high in the hills and was owned by an easygoing man named Kevin. It was a spare space, a space for visitors, a space for people needing somewhere to live or simply in need of a bolt-hole for a while.

When Matt arrived, Kevin was taking a shower. The bathroom had no walls and backed onto the rear wall of his house. Kevin's head was covered in suds and he barely looked around as Matt arrived. Matt saw only a stocky, pale, hairy body, buttocks splattered with froth. "Sure, mate, sure," Kevin said. There was no one using the camper at the moment. He told Matt to *go for your life.* He could stay as long as he liked.

It was an old camper, spare of comforts. There was a gas stove, a double bed. A water tank stood outside, filled by a pipe from Kevin's roof.

There was a view of hills, and acres of forest; it was the kind of country Matt felt familiar with. They'd come here, bringing the baby Emmy carried in her belly, to wait for its arrival. Matt had felt, without expressing it to himself, that this country, and this landscape, would winkle itself into the baby's soul.

He remembered floating in the dark waters of the creek late in the afternoon, sitting out at dawn in front of the camper with a cup of tea, watching the sky, dragging the mattress out to sleep under the stars on hot nights.

The camper was stuffy. Matt opened the windows and spread out a sheet on the double bunk. He lay there and sweated. Mahalia explored the camper and the area outside it. He called to her through the window to make sure she didn't wander too far, but she knew where he was, all right. She came in to clamber all over him, putting her fingers into his mouth. Her needs made themselves felt, as they always did. She wanted food: he fed her on some bread and fruit he'd brought with him. Her diaper was sopping: he took it off and let her run round with a bare bottom. She was soon filthy from playing in the dirt, so he removed the rest of her clothes and sluiced her down with water from the tank, gulping down mouthfuls of the water as he did so, grateful for its coolness. After that she slept, and he was left with his own thoughts.

It was thinking that he didn't want to do. Confused, all he could think of was Emmy's statement that she wanted Mahalia to live with her. *This is your chance for freedom, boy*, he told himself, but it wasn't his own voice he was hearing. It was someone else's, Elijah's maybe, the voice of someone who was more cynical and didn't understand.

Kevin came down and asked Matt up to the house "for a feed," but Matt declined the offer. He couldn't bear the thought of kindness. He needed to be alone. When Mahalia woke, he cooked up some rice with milk and fed her on that. He ate nothing himself; he found he wasn't hungry.

Mahalia

That night it stormed. The wind buffeted the camper and Matt felt it might take off, blow right over the edge of the slope where it perched. He put his face next to Mahalia's, listening to her breath. She whimpered occasionally in her sleep.

In the distance he heard dogs barking. There were other thoughts he was resisting. Of Eliza, the night before. Her arm across his chest. The way she'd whispered, "Just go to sleep."

Matt didn't go to sleep. He lay and listened to the storm and waited for it to pass.

At the birth, when Emmy had finally given the last enormous push that launched Mahalia into the world, she'd gestured to the nurse to give the baby to Matt. So he was the first to hold her, snuggled into his armpit. She'd opened her eyes and looked at him, really looked at him, before closing her eyes and sleeping again. Then Matt took her, swaddled and new, to where Emmy still lay on the delivery table, so that she could see her baby for the first time.

She was a good baby. For the first weeks Mahalia had simply fed and slept, surfacing every so often to feed again. After Emmy fed her, she would lay her beside Matt, and Matt would watch the expressions on her face. Mahalia frowned, and little wrinkles creased themselves across her forehead; she pursed her lips; her eyelids flickered, she smiled a drunken smile. It was as if she were practicing all the expressions she would need throughout her lifetime. She woke herself up momentarily and then sent herself off to sleep again, floating in a state between sleep and consciousness.

Everything smelt milky. Emmy complained of the milk that seeped constantly from her breasts. She tried to wake Mahalia sometimes to get rid of the excess milk, and sometimes she cried with frustration, as Mahalia found it hard to take hold of her nipple. After one week in the hospital and one week in the camper, Matt's mother arrived to visit and took a look at the struggle they were having. She insisted gently that they come and live with her for a while. Matt wanted to refuse, but he saw the look of gratitude on Emmy's face and agreed to go.

It rained all next morning. Mahalia was cranky and bored, and Matt sang songs to soothe her. He cooked rice in powdered milk again and they ate it direct from the saucepan, turn and turn about. *One spoon for you and one for me.* Matt knew he'd need to do something about the food situation. A trip into town seemed necessary, but he didn't want to make it. He still didn't know what he thought, or what he would do, but it felt safe here. He washed out some diapers by hand in Kevin's laundry and hung them on a line strung across one end of the van.

The sun came out early in the afternoon. Matt slung his duffel bag across one shoulder and hoisted Mahalia up into his arms and set off across the hills. He found a stack of pumpkins in a field and put one into his bag and kept walking. The light was clear after the rain, and every color was brilliant and distinct. He tramped on, passing houses, and saw washing flapping from lines. He waved to children who had come out to make the most of the break in the weather. Into the duffel bag he popped several chokoes he found growing over a fence. He felt strong and invincible and absurdly optimistic, stepping over sagging barbed-wire fences, his jeans wet to the knees from the long grass. He had no idea where he was going but simply needed to move. He had Mahalia on his shoulders, exclaiming and waving her arms at the world.

They came at last to a shed of ancient timber and rusty galvanized iron, with one side open to the weather and a sloping, broken wooden floor. A vine with purple trumpet flowers draped itself across the windows.

He was about to go inside and explore but heard a movement at the back, then footsteps, and a moment later came face to face with a young man so tall and wild and thin that he thought for a moment he might be looking in a mirror.

It gave him a shock, the *something* in the young man that reminded him of himself. His eyes were at exactly Matt's height, so Matt looked into them easily, without needing to look down, as he usually did with people.

The man held out his hand and smiled, a shy, diffident smile. "Hello," he said, "I'm Anton."

He was the thinnest person Matt had ever seen. His skin was gray. He looked as if he could do with a good feed. His hair was stiff and dull. Matt put his hand up to his own hair self-consciously. "Hi," he said nervously. "I'm Matt. And this is Mahalia."

Anton smiled. "I don't often get visitors." He gestured toward the wide entrance of the shed. "Do you want to come in?"

Anton showed Matt around. He was proud of what he'd done with the shed. He'd made a rough kind of home of it. It used to be full of junk, he said. All along one wall there was a row of old refrigerators, none of them working, but there was no electricity anyway. Someone brought the fridges here once, he said; he couldn't think why, but here they were, and they served as cupboards for his things.

Since the place didn't have four walls, he'd scrounged enough timber to fill in a little room at one end, and it was here that he slept, away from the wind and the weather. He offered Matt some chokoes from the vine that grew up over the house, perhaps seeing the hunger in his face. Matt took them, not wanting to refuse, though he'd already scrounged chokoes for himself.

Anton showed Matt the way fig trees had germinated in his gutters, in the leaves that had composted there. Matt wondered if they were strangler fig, and imagined them in time enveloping the shed, the way figs did with host trees. Anton looked the sort of person who wouldn't mind that—he'd live somehow between the aerial roots. He had the face of someone who'd been ship wrecked and adrift on a lifeboat for weeks: his skin rough, his hair harsh, eyes staring from a face that looked out at the horizon hopefully, but somehow hopelessly, too, for sight of land.

"George is expecting me," he said suddenly, as if just remembering, "for afternoon tea."

"That sounds very ladylike," Matt blurted out, and Anton laughed, slapping him on the back.

"Will you join us?" said Anton, in a posh accent, and then laughed again.

So, with Mahalia waving her arms and talking to the sky, they headed up the hill to George's place, which was an old farmhouse with all the modern conveniences compared with where Anton was living. But still, it was modest enough, with cracked gray paint on the outside and dull yellow paint on the inside.

Mahalia

George was an old man with mottled old skin and no bum to speak of, so that the seat of his trousers was baggy. They were too big for him, so it seemed that he'd recently lost a lot of weight. Matt thought how he was once a little baby, like Mahalia, with perfect pearly skin and a mother who nibbled on his little toes and marveled at how tiny and perfect his toenails were.

George had made a magnificent afternoon tea of scones he'd freshly baked, with jam and cream and butter, and thick slices of white bread with corned meat and pickles. The minute Matt saw this spread, all laid out at a table with a white cotton cloth embroidered with pansies, the saliva spurted into his mouth, and he swallowed it, and felt ashamed of his greed.

But he needn't have. George was as greedy as Matt, spreading dollops of jam and mountains of cream onto his scones. Mahalia sat on Matt's lap and crammed food into her mouth. Matt realized how hungry he'd been, and almost laughed at the sudden unexpected abundance of it. The four of them ate as if there were no tomorrow, though all the time Matt was mindful of his manners, and he had to drink his tea carefully to avoid spilling the hot liquid onto Mahalia.

Seeing his handicap, George put out his arms to take her, and Mahalia crawled across onto George's lap as if she'd always known him. He jiggled her up and down. "Ah, a baby," he said. "We haven't had one of these here for a while. You looking after her on your own?"

"Yes," said Matt. George nodded, as if he was unsurprised by this.

Anton hadn't said a word while they ate, and now he got up

from the table with a stricken expression on his face and went outside onto the veranda. Matt saw him through the window. He went to a veranda post and, very slowly and rhythmically, started to hit his head against it.

George shook his head and looked at Matt. "He's got his troubles all right. Doesn't say anything about them. I've seen him knock his head against trees, tear at his hair. But it passes. It passes."

George set Mahalia down onto the floor and got up to refill the teapot. "I don't know. He came to live in the shed a while back—asked me if he could fix it up. I try to be kind to him—what else can you do?"

George looked at his carefully set table, with the neat cloth and the bone-china crockery set out just so. He said, "My wife, Marge, she died two years back. But I keep things up. You have to keep going."

He refilled Matt's cup. "You can't drop your bundle," he said. "Can you?"

The days were long, and by the time Matt got back to the camper there were still hours of light left. He looked at the sky. It seemed that the rain would stay away. Matt dumped the chokoes and pumpkin onto the table. They could eat pasta with vegetables for dinner, borrow a few tomatoes from Kevin's garden. Even after the huge afternoon tea Matt was hungry again, and tired after the walk back with Mahalia in his arms.

He took her up to Kevin's bathtub, ran some water in, and popped her in for a proper bath, with soap, washing her hair as well. "You can't drop your bundle, Mahalia," he told her. She grinned back at him and hit the water with the palms of her hands, sending it spraying up into her face.

He wrapped her snugly in a towel he found on Kevin's clothesline. Wherever they were, this was their routine. Bath, then food. It was what he knew. It was what he was good at. He didn't know what he'd do without the weight of her in his life. He whispered his old refrain to her as he toweled her dry. *Bundle of joy. Ball and chain . . .*

Kevin came out of the house with a package in his hands. "Hey, mate," he said. "Charlie killed that pig of his, gave me all these chops. Can you use some?"

Matt cooked them on an improvised barbecue while it was still light. He sat Mahalia on a log, where she wriggled impatiently. He'd slicked her hair down with a comb and she looked scrubbed and tidy. But she couldn't sit still long. She hopped off the log and began running around, still full of energy.

"Hey, Mahalia!"

She stopped and turned to look at him.

"We'll go back tomorrow, hey? Tell your mum that she and I can share looking after you."

When the chops were cooked, Matt put them onto two plates and cut Mahalia's meat up into strips. They ate them with their fingers. Mahalia chewed at each mouthful of meat till there was no juice left in it, then spat it out onto the side of her plate.

"It's good, eh? This is the sort of feed we needed."

Mahalia looked back at him seriously, her fingers poised in the act of picking up the next juicy morsel. It reminded him of the way she'd looked at him when she was born, as if she knew everything. She'd reminded Matt of one of those long-distance swimmers—of that girl who kept getting into a shark-proof cage and swimming all the way between Florida and Cuba. Her face puffy and covered with white, waxy stuff, Mahalia looked as if she'd come a long way. When she looked into Matt's eyes, she seemed as wise as someone who'd been alive for thousands of years.

Now she was thirteen months old. And in that time he felt she'd taught him just about everything he knew.

18

Emmy came over the crest of the hill in the middle of the morning, shielding her eyes from the light with her arm. Matt turned to watch her approach; she squinted from the sun, or from shyness. He was caught by surprise by her unexpected arrival, and didn't know what to say.

Nor did she. They stood staring at each other, shocked by their sudden proximity alone in a place where they'd held so many hopes.

Mahalia's voice, urgent and surprised, came from inside the camper. "You'd better come in," said Matt. The words had an ordinary sound to them, and he said them in a way that wasn't hostile, but he wished they sounded a little more welcoming.

Mahalia was exclaiming about a blue butterfly she'd noticed trapped against the window. Matt pushed the window open and the butterfly blundered its way out. Mahalia cried, her mouth turned down with the disappointment of her loss. "Shh," he said, picking her up and starting to sing one of the songs that Eliza often sang to her. Unwittingly, it called up Eliza to him, with her strong determined walk and her voluptuous way of commanding the space in the kitchen.

"You've learned to sing," said Emmy. Her voice sounded strange. Matt handed Mahalia to her and smiled, his way of making her welcome. Mahalia made no effort to struggle or to get away; Emmy was familiar to her now. She looked up into Emmy's face and smiled, putting her finger to the corner of her mother's mouth. "You funny little thing," Emmy said softly, as if to herself. And then, more loudly, turning Mahalia round to face her squarely, she said, "You're a funny little thing. Do you know that?"

"I thought I might find you here," she said to Matt. "That Eliza girl said you'd just packed up and gone; she didn't know where you'd be. But I kind of guessed."

"It seems a long time since we lived here," said Emmy, her voice wistful. She sat down on the bed and leaned back instinctively, her fingers remembering, and discovered a pair of star-shaped earrings in the corner of the shelf above the bed. She'd always put them there when she slept. She stared at them sadly and then tucked them into the pocket of her jeans. "Funny . . . ," she said.

"What?"

Emmy lay back and closed her eyes. She shrugged. "Nothing."

Matt sat down beside her. Mahalia bounced up and down on Emmy's stomach, laughing, the butterfly forgotten. Emmy, her eyes still closed, winced, but made no effort to push her away.

Emmy was so close Matt could see the buttery texture of her skin, smooth and pale beneath the freckles. Her hip bones protruded above the waistband of her jeans, her stomach a concave hammock between them. He was reminded of how frail she always seemed, her bones too evident under her skin. He felt he could reach out and touch her but he didn't dare. It had been too long now.

He remembered how she used to whisper to him in the night, in the dark, when she thought he was asleep. Her mouth against his back. So soft that she thought he didn't hear. *I love you*, she'd said, so faintly the words were like an expelled breath. When he was with her, he'd become as transparent as glass. The words had drifted onto his back and fogged it up, like a warm breath on a cool window.

Having her so close again was almost unbearable. He remembered things he'd tried for months not to think of.

The first time they'd made love (the sky through the trees, a twig against his buttock, an ant crawling along his arm, but who was noticing?), Matt had stopped suddenly and looked at Emmy, and said brightly, "Hey, do you want to have a baby?"

He'd meant it as sarcasm, as a warning, as a hint that perhaps they should *use something*, but Emmy's face was serious when she said, "I don't mind."

Emmy's face, when he was close to her like that, was different from the face he'd known before. It was her original face, the face she'd had before she'd even existed, before there was any world for her to exist in.

"I don't mind," she'd said, and from then on, though they didn't speak of her, Mahalia was searched for beneath their questing fingers, underneath their skins. Mahalia was something they could *do* with their bodies that no one else (or no one, not even themselves) had any control over.

Once, Matt found his body patterned with the imprint of grass; he had lain so long with Emmy asleep on top of him, her head on his shoulder—a whole afternoon. A tick wandered along her thigh, drawn perhaps by the whiteness of her skin and the warmth of her naked body.

They were both so thin that their hipbones clashed. Emmy tasted saltily of the sea that he felt sure she must have come from in another life, and when he stroked her freckled back he imagined colors playing beneath her skin, rose pink and sky blue, moving in waves, and a silvery iridescence pulsating in time with her breath.

He was relieved when she slid away from him and off the bed to stand in the doorway of the camper. She went outside, and he followed a few moments later with Mahalia and found her looking out toward the distant hills. The rain had cleared the air and made everything sharply defined—the hills, the high wisps of white cloud, and the leaves on the trees. Even Emmy's face in profile was so clear against the blue of the sky that Matt felt he could reach out a finger and run it down the outline that separated Emmy from the rest of the world.

When they lived here in the camper, Emmy had rubbed her expectant belly with oil; he remembered the shape of it, heavy, like a raindrop about to fall. Or like a piece of fruit, her belly button the place where the stalk had come away. They had both been expectant then, expectant with hope and full of idealism.

Now, against the clarity of the sky, she said: "I was too young. We were both too young. We shouldn't have had her."

Tears spurted suddenly and unexpectedly into Matt's eyes, blinding him. "Don't *say* that," he cried out. "Don't *say that!*" Mahalia, startled by the anguish in his voice and the sudden tension in his body, started to wail. Matt turned his face away so that Emmy couldn't see him; his nose was dripping suddenly and he wiped it with the back of his hand.

"I'm sorry," said Emmy. "I'm really sorry."

Matt said, "I'm not. I'm glad we had her." His love for Mahalia was so pure and heavy that he thought he'd faint.

He caught hold of one of her feet; she stopped crying and her toes curled up with pleasure as he grasped her foot firmly. The weight of her in his arms reassured him. "Let's sit down," he said.

He and Emmy sat cross-legged on the ground, facing each other. Mahalia squirmed out of Matt's grasp and went away to explore.

"There's no chance of us getting together again, is there," said Matt. It wasn't a question.

Emmy shook her head. "It's gone past that."

"I know." Still, Matt felt sad. He glanced across to where Mahalia was picking up stones and looking at them. She was the one he had to think of now.

"You should have seen her the first time she walked," he said. "I might easily have missed it, but I was there." He smiled at the memory. "She was holding herself up with this bloody laundry basket and pushing it along. And then she saw me and let go. . . ."

He felt the beginnings of tears in his eyes but he blinked them away. He refused to cry.

"I'm sorry I missed all that," said Emmy. "But I'm back now."

Matt nodded grimly, staring at the ground as he spoke. "I just want you to explain," he said slowly, "why you went away."

"I'll try," said Emmy.

"Going down to stay with Charlotte—you know, my god-mother—really helped me. I could tell her things I couldn't even tell you."

Matt looked up at her. "Like what?"

A defensive expression appeared on her face; Matt was startled to see that she was afraid to tell him.

"What?" he repeated gently.

Emmy's expression became determined. "Well, like when Mahalia was born, I felt really ashamed because I didn't fall in love with her the way you did. She was just this little bundle that cried and ate and pissed and wanted too much from me. And you're supposed to love your baby, aren't you? Everyone says so. But Charlotte reckons that's just a myth. She said she didn't fall in love with her second baby till he was about a year old. Lots of women feel like that, she says."

"And now you feel better about her and you want her back," said Matt hoarsely. Emmy didn't reply.

"Well," he said, "I'm sorry you got depressed and couldn't handle having her. And I'm sorry I couldn't help you more at the time but you never really said what you were feeling. I don't know. I thought you were just tired from looking after her or something, and I tried to do my bit." He got to his feet and went over to look out at the valley laid out below.

"So what will you do with yourself?" he asked, turning his head. "Any plans?"

"Yeah!" Emmy went over to him, her hands in the pockets of her jeans. "I want to go back to school. Do Year 12." She swept her arms out wide, embracing the whole valley that stretched below them like a model landscape. "And then—the sky will be my limit. I could go to uni, become a vet, or a famous racehorse trainer. . . ."

"I'll live with my parents for a while," she said more soberly, "while I finish school. Staying with Charlotte was great. Helped me work out a lot of things. Do you know what? I was wrong in thinking I was adopted. Charlotte says that Mum and Dad tried for ages to have a baby, and then finally, when Mum was forty-two and had given up all hope, she got pregnant. Charlotte says that's why they always fussed over me too much and made me feel stifled. I always hated how *old* they were compared with everyone else's parents. . . ."

She caught sight of Mahalia, who was sitting on the ground, putting stones into an old plant pot she'd found.

"Hey, Mahalia!" Emmy called. Mahalia looked up, and Emmy ran across to her and crouched in front of her. With a mischievous look on her face, Emmy began to tickle Mahalia's bare sole and then walk her fingers up Mahalia's leg. "Incy-wincy spider, coming to get you . . ."

Mahalia watched, smiling, mesmerized. Matt felt the familiar wave of pain pass through his body and reach the top of his head. Emmy could charm anybody. And if she thought she could just come back and take Mahalia away from him . . .

His world swung in an arc.

Blue. Green. Brown. The red of Emmy's shirt.

He swooped and seized Mahalia, holding her tightly against him. She squawked with surprise. Her breath was sweet and intoxicating.

Emmy's face. Dark sprinkling of freckles. Eyes, looking into his. *No crying.* His breath shuddered. Emmy's cool fingers were against his cheek. Her white pale slender fingers.

"Don't *look* like that," she said, sounding frightened.

"Like what?"

She didn't reply, just kept looking at him. Mahalia wriggled to get free and he released her onto the ground.

Matt stared into Emmy's face earnestly, willing her to understand how he felt. "I *am* sorry you went through a hard time after she was born. But I was the one who looked after her when you went away and I did a good job of it. I'm *good* at looking after her. It's one thing I do *really well*. I won't let you take her away from me!"

Emmy laughed, embarrassed by his vehemence.

"Well, I *am*. I know your parents think I'm hopeless, but . . . look at her." He gestured toward Mahalia. "She's healthy . . . and happy. . . ."

"But I'm her *mother*!" Emmy put her hands on her hips.

"So? Nothing will change that."

"I could take it to court!"

There was silence. The whole world seemed shocked. Then cicadas started a rhythmic thrumming in the trees. Matt looked over at Mahalia; she had filled the plant pot with stones and now she was tipping them out onto the ground again.

"And you'd probably win," he said quietly. "Just because you are her mother. We both know the way things are set up. But you don't want to do that, do you?"

"No," said Emmy defensively.

Matt felt that they'd made a mess of things. From now on he could only salvage something. He thought of his father and the long trail of uncertainty that could be drawn through a life. "I want Mahalia to grow up knowing both of us," he said. "Spending lots of time with both of us. That's what a kid wants. But you went away and she's used to living with me," he said. "She's too young to go chopping and changing now."

Emmy looked squarely into his eyes.

"So that's why she should stay with me," said Matt.

"Emmy?" he said, trying to get through to her. "Let her keep living with me. For now, anyway. I don't want to take her away from you—I'd never do that. . . . But she's her own person. Getting more that way every day. Maybe one day she'll want to go and live with you. I think that's quite likely." A lump filled his throat. "I could handle that."

"Could you?" said Emmy, and laughed bitterly.

"Maybe," said Matt. Not having Mahalia with him was as unimaginable to him as his own death.

Emmy looked at him steadily. "Well, I suppose you *deserve* her more," she said. "At least, a lot of people would see it that way. But I can't just go away and forget about her, you know. I've thought of nothing else for months. I need to be able to have her sometimes. More than just sometimes. I want her to be a real part of my life."

The words hung between them. Some words, like music, require space to make themselves felt.

"Yes," said Matt at last. "I know. But can we go on as we've been doing, for now?"

"Okay," said Emmy. "For now. But I want to work out something we can all live with."

Matt nodded. For now. That would have to do.

Mahalia's cries interrupted them. She'd fallen over, and she wanted attention. Matt strode over to where she sat wailing on

the ground and, scooping her up, returned to Emmy. All three of
them sat down on the ground together.

"She likes horses too," Matt said. "Don't you?" he added,
addressing the last remark to Mahalia.

"Horse!" she said, bouncing up and down on his lap.

Emmy grinned reluctantly at him. "Remember," she said,
"when you held her for the first time? The smell of your armpit
was her first experience of the world."

Matt felt for a long, optimistic moment that even though he
and Emmy mightn't be together, they could somehow do the best
for their baby, somehow make it all work. He knew this was just the
beginning of years of compromise and negotiations and juggling
their time with her, but he wanted to make it work, for Mahalia.

He reached out quickly and took Emmy's hand. It was fine and
weightless and pale. He glanced briefly at the constellation of
freckles across her nose, and without passion, but for old times'
sake, he kissed the top of her hand quickly and laid it against his
cheek for a moment before letting it go again.

Because Matt *had* loved Emmy, with her freckled, luminous,
magical body; he had loved the way she hadn't given a damn for
anything, the way she had climbed onto the roof of the church
tower and kissed and kissed him. The way she'd fallen into the
river *just to know what it felt like*. He had loved the way she'd said
to her parents, "We'll just love it, okay?"

He remembered how they had believed that loving Mahalia
would be enough.

Matt packed up their things, glancing round as he did so and imprinting the place on his memory, for he knew he'd never return. Then Emmy drove them back to town; she said she wouldn't stay but would come and see Mahalia tomorrow. Matt stood and watched her drive away, Mahalia on his hip. Mahalia waved until the car was out of sight. Then Matt found his key, picked up their meager belongings, and opened the door. When it swung shut, it echoed with a comforting familiar sound.

No one was at home. Inside was cool and dark and quiet. Matt made his way up the stairs to his yellow room and set Mahalia down onto the floor. He made up her crib, ready for bed (soon she would be needing a real bed, and her own room). He opened the door out onto his balcony and leaned over the railing; he could see Virginia way down at the end of the street, recognizing her familiar shambling gait before he noticed her face beneath her hat. She saw him watching and waved. Matt waved back, then noticed the tangled wind chimes he'd thrown into a corner of the veranda. He hung them up again, where they resumed their bony pensive sound.

It was all so ordinary. So ordinary and familiar and good.

He went downstairs and looked in the cupboards at the food situation. There were dried lentils and pasta and potatoes and baked beans in the cupboard; milk and cheese and yogurt and a squeaky fresh half cabbage in the fridge. He was in the kitchen making dinner when he heard the front door bang shut.

Every one of her footsteps resounded in his head as she strode from the front door, *one, two, three, four, five, six, seven*, and down the tiny hall to the kitchen, *eight, nine, ten*.

The footsteps stopped.

Matt turned around from the stove.

Eliza smiled, staring at the floor, not at him. She grabbed a scrap of raw cabbage from the chopping board, crunching it between her teeth. "So you're back," she said.

Weeks later, on a cool sunny day, Matt and Eliza set out on their bikes. Even though he'd got his permit at last and started to learn to drive, Matt had brought his bike in from his mother's place. With Mahalia in a baby seat on the back, they rode out of Lismore the hard way, up the steep hill that led to the coast.

They rode to a rainforest remnant for a "small forest walk" that Matt knew of. There was a grassy park outside the forest, and the rainforest was tiny, not big enough to get lost in, not really big enough to even walk in for very long. It wasn't like the rainforest where Matt had grown up. It was a tame forest, a forest for tourists, to give them a taste of what the "big scrub" that once covered the north coast had been like.

When they arrived in the parking lot with their bikes, Matt saw a man and a boy getting out of a car. The boy was about fourteen or fifteen, and they were obviously father and son, they looked so alike. The car was an old sports car, a single man's car, and something about them made Matt feel that perhaps the two didn't live together, that they were on a visit with each other. Matt took Mahalia out of her bike seat and unstrapped her helmet as he watched them walk away into the forest.

There was a playground in the park, and instead of going off on a walk right away, he and Eliza decided to rest and let Mahalia play there.

"You're thoughtful," observed Eliza, narrowing her golden eyes against the sun. She lay on her back on the grass, lolling like a big cat.

"Am I?" said Matt. He sat beside her, cross-legged, and tore a leaf into strips. "What did you mean when you said that you thought we're all a long way from home?"

Eliza looked astonished. "I must have said that ages ago! Fancy you remembering that!"

"I remember lots of things."

"When was it?"

"That time in the kitchen when I played the guitar and you sang. What did you mean?"

"You do have a good memory."

"Well?"

"It's just this feeling I have that lots of people aren't in the place where they really feel at home. You can spend a lifetime searching for it. I never truly felt at home with my family—I was always way different from them, even though I love them. Maybe for lots of people the only place they'll ever be at home is in heaven. But I like to feel that I'll find a home somewhere here on earth."

Mahalia, who had been playing a little way off, came over to them and flopped onto Eliza's lap. Eliza reached into her bag and took out an orange and peeled it with her fingers, giving a segment to Matt and one to Mahalia.

"Sometimes," said Eliza, "I feel at home for brief moments, in a particular place, at a particular time. Like now. Maybe that's all you can hope for."

Matt smiled across at her. "I feel at home when I'm playing with the band," he said. He thought of the other night when he'd played his first gig with them at a pub. He thought he'd be nervous in front of a crowd of people, but once the music had started, he'd flowed right with it.

The father and son had come back from their walk now, and sat together on the grass under a tree, cross-legged, next to each other but not facing. Like Matt, they had each picked up a leaf and were tearing them to bits, perhaps as an aid to concentration. There was an intimacy between them that Matt envied.

It hadn't been great, that time he'd seen his father. But Matt felt that he was old enough now to make overtures he couldn't make before, be the first one to make a move, even if his father couldn't. Just as long as he didn't expect too much. It was the gesture that was important. In his head he composed the letter he'd write to his father, telling him about Mahalia, sending him some photos, perhaps.

Matt felt luxurious, having the whole day with Eliza and Mahalia stretched ahead of him. His mother had once said that earth was the right place for love, quoting some poet or other. She was right. It was. Trees, grass, sky, birds, soft, warm air caressing your body . . . It was a friendly planet to be alive on, a kind planet, and one where you *could* love, if that luxury came your way.

Mahalia

"What do you want for Mahalia?" Eliza said suddenly. "You know, if a good fairy arrived to bestow graces on her."

Matt considered her question, but he didn't need to think for long.

"Oh," he said, "all the ordinary things that parents want for their children. That she grow up strong and healthy and happy."

Eliza put another piece of orange into his mouth. He savored its sweetness.

"I want her to be confident and unafraid . . . to find something that she really loves to do, that she's good at. You know, not just a *job* to make money . . . some kind of passion . . ."

Eliza sucked on a piece of orange carefully, sucking the juice out from one end. Matt watched her mouth, the keen movement of her white teeth. He could kiss her now, he thought. Before, the memories of Emmy were too raw for him, but now . . .

Matt laughed, though he wasn't sure why. He jumped to his feet and put out a hand to pull her up to face him. He kissed her lightly on the mouth and said, "Come on, let's go and get lost in this rainforest."

Eliza peeled another orange and they wandered toward the entrance of the walk, with Mahalia trotting along between them. Then, with their arms around each other, and Mahalia on Eliza's hip, they disappeared into the cool darkness of the forest. There was no sound except for their soft footsteps on the fallen leaves, and a bird calling, and a jet plane flying high overhead. They crammed the last of the orange into their mouths and smiled at each other, and the juice ran down their chins.

JOANNE HORNIMAN has spent most of her life in rural New South Wales, apart from a few years in Sydney and some time traveling overseas. She has worked as an editor, teacher, and artist—some of the posters she helped produce are in the print collection of the National Gallery of Australia. She lives outside Lismore in a house and workshop she and her partner built themselves, and has two sons. Everyone in the family plays music, apart from Joanne, and she says, "The rural peace is sometimes shattered by teenage boys jamming in the workshop." As well as writing and reading, she likes to propagate rainforest trees, practice yoga, grow vegetables, and walk along the beach.